# Never too Late

Prof. G. K. MITHAL

# Never too Late

Prof. G. K. MITHAL

pblishing.com
write · share · connect · publish

**Never too Late** *by* **Prof. G. K. Mithal**



**Published by www.pblishing.com**

**Marketed by**

**Maple Press Private Limited**
**sales office** : A 63, Sector 58, Noida 201 301, U.P., India
**phone** : +91 120 455 3581, 455 3583
**email** : info@maplepress.co.in
**website** : www.maplepress.co.in

**ISBN** : 978-81-93324-84-4
**Cover, Layout, Typesetting, and Book Design** : Flying Trees Private Limited
**Inside Illustrations** : Smitha

10 9 8 7 6 5 4 3 2 1

*Dedicated to*

**LOVE**

•••

# FOREWORD

Early in 2015, my mother recovered a small box that belonged to my grandfather. We had changed cities right after his death and the box had gotten untraceable amongst the many goods that had to be transported using a total of nine cargo trucks. The box contained quite a few half-finished manuscripts of various genres such as comedy and history, and one finished manuscript titled "Never Too Late" that my *dadaji* (grandfather) had written during the nineties.

My father took it upon himself to get this book printed, and started the initial process of identifying editors and printers. His sudden demise in 2015 temporarily stalled this process. I then picked up the project to fulfil my father's dream of seeing his father's work in print. In 2017, Pblishing.com enabled me to crowd-fund this book and get it published. Though it was after a gap of seventeen years, yet I believe that it was 'Never Too Late' to see this in its final form.

My grandfather had passed away in the year 2000. I still miss him; and my dad too.

This is for both of them!

-Saurabh

# CHAPTER 1

**Seth Dina Nath** was a business tycoon of real estate industry. He lived in his ancestral home, which was to the west of Ghaziabad, in Rampur, way outside New Delhi. He was a happy, middle aged man with a daughter, Pramela, born to him and his wife in their mid-forties. Pramela was their only child.

It was when **Pramela** was four months old, the occasion of her '*ann prascna*' (when the child is fed semi solid food for the first time) was held. A huge *pandaal* (tent) was set up in the lawn that was covered with thick mattresses and chairs; occupied by business associates, friends and the extended family.

Seth Dina Nath was dressed in an exquisite white *kurta* (dress for men) that day, beaming with happiness. His wife, Sarla Devi wore a *banarasi* Silk *saree* (dress for women) with gold embroidery and an ornate matching blouse. She was also decked with gold jewellery. Pramela, Seth Dina Nath's daughter was dressed in a cream colour silk frock that he had bought himself.

**Pandit Dev Swaroop**, the officiating priest from a society known as the Arya Samaj, was cladd in a spot less white *kurta* and *dhoti* with a scarf around his neck. He chanted Sanskrit mantras and also explained the same in Hindi for the people to understand their meaning. He then started the '**havan**' by placing an iron pot on the bricks. The pot was lined with dry wood chips of the mango tree. He lit the wood and made fire; then started to chant the *shlokas* (Mythical verses) and put the *aahuti* (a mixture of some cereals, *ghee*, nuts and scrap of few other things) in small amounts into the pot of fire as an offering, followed immediately by the customary '*Swaha!*' at end of every *shloka*. The ceremony went on for a while and then a '*purna aahuti*' (final offering into the pot of fire) was given with the remaining mixture along with the flowers. Flower petals were distributed to all those present, and all guests joined in the final offerings ritual. Finallly flowers were showered on the baby by everyone; blessing her with a long, healthy and prosperous life.

While the ceremony was still on, there were a few guests who were not interested in the ceremony and were thus getting bored. These guests were of considerable consequence in business deals, but they were also the people at the periphery of the acquaintance circle of Seth Dina Nath. They were neither relatives nor close friends or officials, but people who were always invited in functions arranged by dignitaries. The deliberations in progress were not of any consequence to them. Naturally in such cases, silence becomes too noisy and perturbing! They must thus engage themselves in some conversation; weather politics, local scandals or sometime pertaining to the news related with their hosts. Mr. Singh was in automobile business and made good money with honesty and integrity. He could no longer restrain himself, and said to the people sitting near him, "You know, over thousand people will be dining here, apart from cateress, servants and others. No one spends his hard earned money so lavishly over other people," he exclaimed.

"What exactly do you want to say Mr. Singh, please elaborate," said Mrs. Kohli, who was seated just next to Mr. Singh, and was famous for her gossip and pungent tongue.

"You all know, Mr. Dina Nath is flourishing by manipulating money of the investors. If the shares go up, he is the major gainer and the investor only the minor one. On the other hand, if the shares go down, he disowns his responsibility," said Mr. Singh. "But that is what everyone does; the investor has to take more caution in going through the instructions. No one can blame the broker for market fluctuations," said Mrs. Kohli with an intention of prolonging the conversation and at the same time putting up a show to defend Mr. Dina Nath, her host.

"There is no moral left in business today. Gone are those days when we could rely on someone," commented Mr. Singh. "That is true for all. Money has become very important. Moral values have completely eroded. Look at our politicians. A bunch of power and money hungry lot," said Mrs. Kohli.

Suddenly there was murmur and people started getting up from their seats. The final oblation was over and every one blessed the child by showering flowers at her. The priest blew the conch, signalling that the ceremony was over. This was followed by a series of short lectures by eminent persons, the relatives of Seth Dina Nath and the family. Each person took about 2 to 5 minutes to give blessings to the baby girl.

The public address system had been installed so that all could listen to the orations. This was followed by announcement of donations given by Seth Dina Nath to various sanatan dharma and arya samaj temples, educational institutions, destitute homes and old age residences.

Thereafter announcement was made inviting people to the buffet counters set for lunch. Food was laid on the tables along the boundary of the lawn and well liveried bearers served the food; hot and spicy, pure vegetarian and lavishly prepared in both quality and variety.

The host, the relatives and the close friends with their family waited. The others were to dine first. The first diners were the people who made the maximum use of their time; last to come and first to dine and leave!

Then there were those nicknamed 'the experienced ones', that is the people who often attend such ceremonies surveying the arrangements of tables and layout of crockery, etc upon their arrival; and as soon as the rituals get over they inconspicuously and deftly drifted to the table and started to stuff their plates to full capacity with numerous items of their choice. Subsequently the others joined the buffet queues too. The meal having finished, people took leave of Seth Dina Nath, expressing their thanks to him and blessing the child again.

Deewan Harbans Lal along with his band of associates supervised the function and serving of the food ensuring that everyone was taken care of. By the time the last group finished its lunch, it was past 3 pm. Since it was Sunday, a holiday, therefore most of the invitees could attend the function.

Seth Dinanath, soon after everyone left, retired to this bedroom to take some rest and the post function wind-up work continued. Those who stayed on formed groups and talked about the function and other non-related stuff and simultaneously took rest. Most of these groups were formed by the relatives and close associates. The instructions were to not leave before the evening tea and only then depart with parting gifts. A few of the friends from the neighbouring towns were likely to stay overnight. It was overall a good get-together of people closely and distantly related. Many did not know much about others and hence it was a good time to get acquainted with each other. The fabrics of kinship get stronger on such occasions.

Among the relatives who greeted the occasion, was Mrs. Radha. She was in her late forties. She was a second cousin of Seth Dina Nath and was addressed as *bua* (father's sister) by everyone. Radha became a childless widow at an early age. She had, however, made peace with her loneliness and would visit any relative, near or distant, on every occasion, be it child birth, *ann prasana*, (naming ceremony), *yagyopaveet* (thread ceremony), engagement ceremony, marriage or death. She was almost always invited or informed about the function and she would invariably present herself well in time, and take responsibilities of the things that needed to be done, rituals to be performed, donation to be given, etc. She was competent and as such an asset on such occasions. Young ladies of the house usually ignorant of the traditions found solace in inviting her and taking her advice. Her word was taken as the law. She was liberal in rendering services too. On festive occasions she would reach the relevant house a week or two before and would stay well over a month or more. She would then vanish as hastily as her arrival. She had a keen sense of judging the feelings of her host family. Whenever she realized that an indifference was building towards her prolonged stay, she would leave on some pretext or the other. She had a tremendous capacity for work even at this age and that was one factor that made her useful to people. Her attitude towards the relatives was extremely warm and she could engage everyone in conversation. And in her leisure time she would keep company with children of all ages and also with elderly people by sharing the tales of people she knew. Nothing escaped her attention and hence with a little probing one could know all about the love affairs in or outside the family, or about who flirted with whom. Not to mention; she would smoothly mix facts with fancies making episodes more engrossing and palatable. But she could, at the same time, digest with perfection, any serious scandal, and huge amount of cajoling would also not make her part with the truth then. This was one reason why people in distress would take her in confidence and seek her advice.

People, in general, were not aware of her antecedents except a few of her relatives, including Seth Dina Nath. She had led a turbulent life, full of struggles and misery, but at the same time, a life full of achievements and good will to people too. She was a distant cousin to Seth Dina Nath; her father being a man of poor financial standing. Radha's father's greatest worry was to get his daughter married, and he was in constant look out for a suitable match for her. All the relatives assisted him in looking for a groom for Radha, but to find a good match of a suitable background and well settled in life involved considerable amount of dowry. Time passed on and Radha remained unmarried for well past the age that was considered suitable for marriage. She studied only until middle school and that was far beyond that was considered suitable for the family of her means and standing also.

Sarla Devi, Radha's aunt, was a frequent visitor to the family and constantly made Radha's father feel guilty for not having found a match for her. As time progressed, it became obvious that Radha would not get a young groom. But to let a daughter remain unmarried was considered a sin; marriage was must, irrespective of the suitability of the match. One morning, Sarla Devi called Radha's father and suggested a match for Radha; a man of middle age, a widower, with no liabilities and a man well placed in life with a good income. There was no demand of dowry from the groom's family; rather he was willing to bear all the expenses of the marriage. After a prolonged discussion, Sarla Devi convinced Radha's father to accept the proposal. Radha had no choice or say in the matter. For her, and everyone else, it was better for her to be married to this man than to remain unmarried and be a subject of constant ridicule. Having considering all these aspects, the matter was finalized after a formal visit by the bridegroom to see Radha and get her consent. She had no option than to agree to the marriage. All her dreams of getting married to a man of her choice were shattered. She never aspired for a rich or highly educated match but all she wanted, as is true for young girls her age, was a young, healthy and good looking match. But with poise and fortitude she accepted her destiny. The marriage was duly solemnized and Radha went to her husband Mohan Lal's house. He was the head of the family, which consisted of his aged mother and his younger brother and his family. It was a big, residential, two storied house. Radha and Mohan stayed on the ground floor while the rest lived on the upper floor.

Time moved on and Radha adjusted herself in the family.

She had initially no liking for her frail and aged husband, Mohan, on the other hand, adored his wife and took care of everything possible in order to meet all her wishes. He was well educated having secured a Bachelor's degree in Arts and was a good business man. He was an advocate for 'education for women', though he did not want women to take up jobs or pursue a profession. Radha had already studied till the middle school and Mohan encouraged her to study further. In spite of the opposition by other members of the family, he engaged a lady teacher to coach Radha at their residence for appearing in the High School Examination as a private candidate. Radha was intelligent and took on this opportunity. She worked hard and succeeded in passing the High School Certificate Examination with reasonably good marks.

It was now over fifteen years that she was married, but she was not blessed with a child despite all the medical advice and treatment. Yet she quietly made peace with the situation. But the greatest shock of her life was when one morning Mohan succumbed to a massive heart attack and could not be revived. Radha had become a widow!

As per the tradition in those days, Radha was not to wear any jewellery or colourful clothes and was only to wear a white *saree* at all times. The cremation got over and various other formalities were in progress. All relatives were informed about the final ritual to be done on the thirteenth day from the date of cremation. Radha's brother in-laws and all other relatives took over the management of the family. It was discussed that Radha, having become a widow, would have to shave her head as per the age old tradition.

This she resisted to the annoyance of all. She did not want to displease all relatives, but this was beyond her acceptance. She was educated and was aware of the changes in the social customs and rights and duties of a widow in the family. However, all her relative had taken it for granted that Radha would be treated like any other widow; a cursed woman having committed the sin of out-living her husband and was, therefore, to lead a life of perpetual mourning and expiation. The more orthodox ones suggested for her to be confined to a small, dingy room and to live on plain bread and lentils, ordained from good things in life. This was customary a generation or two ago.

There was also a financial angle that needed to be discussed. By confining Radha to a life of penance, her brother-in-law automatically would become the head of the family and the owner of all the business and wealth of this deceased brother. However, Radha had no intention of letting this happen. But the pressure was mounting and she was getting weaker in her struggle with every passing day. The situation, however, changed when Seth Dina Nath came to attend the final ritual on the thirteenth day. As was customary, there was the usual *puja* (Prayer) and *havan.* Prayer for the deceased soul was conducted by making offerings to the fire by eleven Brahmins, followed by a meal and *dakshina* (offerings of money, clothes and utensils) for all the Brahmins, and donation set aside to be given to the temple, the school, and the *anathalaya* (orphanage). Finally all the relatives and other invitees had their meal and one by one paid regards to the family and left. Only the close relatives stayed back in the house and once again the topic regarding the future of Radha came under discussion. At this juncture, Seth Dina Nath strongly supported Radha and ensured that his words were followed as law! Radha was finally the owner of all the business and property that belonged to her deceased husband. Everyone was unhappy but could not challenge the verdict. The law of the country also gave full right to the widows by then. Since there was no child, the entire property went to Radha. It was for Radha to decide how to take care of the assets.

Dina Nath then suggested to her, "You are an educated woman and you may run the business yourself but since you are new to this industry, you may incur losses and that may hit you financially."

"What should I do, please suggest and I shall abide by your advice," said Radha.

"Under this situation, a course of moderation may be good. I suggest you sell the business as it is and put the proceeds in fixed deposits in the bank. The income from interest will be sufficient for your living. It will not be as remunerative as the business but you will certainly avoid the risk of losses and also the associated headache," said Dina Nath.

To this Radha readily agreed. "What about the house?" asked Radha.

Seth Dina Nath thought for a moment and then remarked, "Much depends on your feelings towards your relatives, especially your brother-in-law and his family. It will be too harsh to ask them to leave." So she decided to let the upper floor of the house on rent to her brother-in-law after a written agreement in order to avoid any litigation in future.

The decision was conveyed to all. Radha's mother-in-law was to stay with her. Thus the tables were fully turned and Radha became the sole beneficiary, while the rest, not so well off, were to always remain dependent on her.

It so worked out that Radha was able to live comfortably on less than half of the interest income and thus saved something every month. With the savings she visited her other relatives in the city and also travelled elsewhere.

There was thus a radical transformation in Radha's social status, which she started to enjoy. She did think about her past, about her married life with her husband. She, no doubt, missed him, but also found compensating pleasure in her new found liberty. She had engaged servants for all the domestic chores including cooking. She would occasionally prepare a dish or two of her own liking or that of her mother-in-law's. To her great surprise the attitude of her mother-in-law was now totally changed. She had become very docile and missed no opportunity to please Radha. She knew now which side of the bread to butter! Even greater were the changes in the attitudes of her brother-in-law, Sudhir, and her sister in law Shalini. They had also grasped the reality of the situation and would talk to Rahda very politely and with due respect. Often they sent her some specially prepared dish to please her.

Time passed comfortably. Life was good and Radha grew plump and authoritative. For her, there was no dearth of company; her brother's family and that of her husband were continuous visitors. She would behave amicably; entertain the relatives lavishly; and enjoyed it herself. It was now well accepted by one and all that she was the master of what was hers. She wore the finest of clothes and ate the best food. She would sit in her house and talk to them when she felt and would listen to their takes regarding dearth of money. Sometimes she did them little favours and expected to be praised for the same.

But even this life of prosperity did not give her complete satisfaction. She knew no one really loved her. It was her money and her generous ways to helping in pressing needs of her relatives that endeared her to them. Hence, despite her comfortable situation, she was often restless for periods extending several days. She felt something missing; felt that justice had been denied to her by God. She would then eat and sleep more than usual, not for pleasure but out of compulsion. At such times she would refuse all visitors except one who would continue to stay despite her refusal and would sit reverently by her bed. Her aunt, Sarla Devi, was an occasional visitor and was dearly welcomed. On one such occasion, when Radha was in a bad mood, Sarla Devi happened to visit. She asked Radha as to what was killing her. "Finding a real well-wisher," Radha unburdened herself complaining about the irony of her fate, and about her perpetual dissatisfaction with life. Sarla Devi consoled her to the best of her ability, with carefully considered choice of words; and advised her to put up with the situation with fortitude.

"But what should I do? I am continuously tormented. I never got any real pleasure while my husband was alive, and now, in-spite of this new found freedom, I have no satisfaction," exclaimed Radha.

"God has been cruel to you, no doubt. But what cannot be cured has to be endured, so is the old saying. My advice to you my dear Radha is to make peace in your mind and make the best use of the situation God has put you in. Do pray to God and you will find peace of mind. Be good to people, but do not expect anything in return," said Sarla.

"Shall I go to the temple every day to pray and donate money to the beggars sitting in rows there? Will it get me my peace?" asked Radha.

"Yes, do it if you possess a desire to do it," said Sarla Devi. "Go to *anathalaya* (destitute children's home), talk to them, offer what you can give; money, food, clothes etc. Try to derive pleasure out of it. You stand to gain more than what you give."

"What else should I do?" asked Radha.

"Well, change your life pattern," said Sarla Devi. "Get up early in the morning, take bath and pray to God here in the house itself, remove all worldly thoughts from you mind, make it blank and concentrate on God, in any form you desire, shapeless or statue, or an idol of God, say Ram or Krishna or any God you worship. It will be difficult initially but with practice you may increase your time of meditation. You will find the pleasure. Go to the temple or other places as and when possible."

Sarla Devi then departed with a promise to come again soon. Radha resolved to give the advice a try. She was accustomed to getting up late in the morning. But now she would get up early and get ready for meditation after offering her prayer to the God. But concentration was difficult to come. All sorts of thoughts would constantly crowd her mind. Nevertheless she continued to practice meditation. In the evening she would go to the nearby temple; participate in the worship, talk to other devotees and the Pandit.

But even these regular visits to the temple did not give her peace of mind. Meanwhile a renowned priest from Haridwar, *Pandit* Brahmanand was to conduct religious discourse for ten days in her city. A committee was formed to ensure suitable arrangements for his stay, recourses etc. Radha donated freely for the cause and hence was requested to be on the managing committee. It was a welcome change for her, a deviation from her routine. A week passed by in these hectic activities. Radha came in contact with several philanthropists on the managing committee and also other social workers. At length Swamiji arrived and was lodged in the spacious guest house on the outskirt of the city. The owner of the guest house was a rich business man of the town and had generously offered his home for the occasion. The guest house was well maintained with air conditioned, well-furnished rooms with all modern facilities, spacious well maintained lawns and a band of servants and other staff for its up keep and to provide necessary facilities to the guests. Radha had visited the guest house several times in the week before the arrival of Swamiji. It was a major event in the town and everyone looked forward to have a darshan of the swami and to listen to his preaching.

The train full of disciples arrived early in the morning.

It was a Sunday. A huge crowd of disciples and other people gathered on the railway platform. A commotion ensued as the train came to a halt. Volunteers took care of the luggage etc. while dignitaries put garlands on the Swamiji and his associates. A fleet of cars waited at the railway station for their conveyance. Swamiji was thus accorded a very hearty welcome and was taken to the guest house. Everything went on smoothly. People were not allowed to meet Swamiji just then. In the evening he arrived at the site for the religious discourse with a train of associates and local disciples in attendance. He was a good orator; with a firm command on language and an excellent way of narrating things. The audience heard him in perfect silence broken only at intervals by short *bhajans* (prayers). The entire proceedings lasted for about 3 hours. The same routine continued for a whole week.

It was on the third day that Radha accompanied Swamiji to the guest house. Only very few people were permitted to enter the guest house. Swamiji then retired to his personal suite. Radha ensured that all the necessary arrangements for the next day had been made and was then due to leave for her home. On the spur of moment she thought of taking leave of Swamiji and pay her parting homage for the day. She knocked on the door; as was the usual custom, waited for a while and then entered. What she saw was shocking to her beyond belief! Swamiji was seated on the well cushioned deewan in a half inclined position, embracing an extremely beautiful young lady. Radha turned around to depart quickly but Swamiji called her back. There was no sign of remorse on his face.

Kamla was the name of the lady who was with Swamiji.

She was extremely rich and a social magnate, but was now seeking peace of mind and had decided to lead a life of penance and in worship of God. Kamla had decided to entrust the business management to the manager and be a disciple of Swamiji. Radha had heard about her but did not know her too well. Now the true picture of Swamiji and Kamla had emerged before Radha. She had heard people talk in whispers concerning the weakness of Swamiji for young girls, but had discounted all that as malicious attempts to discredit a great soul.

Swamiji commented, "Kamla has decided to devote her life for religious cause, worship of God and service of mankind."

Radha could not speak and remained rooted to the spot quietly. Eventually Swamiji revealed his thoughts, "A true devotee offers his or her entire self to God or his incarnation. I am an incarnation of God. One, who pleases me, pleases the God."

The philosophy, however, did not appeal to Radha. She was not highly educated, but had read a lot. To her Swamiji appeared to be a fraud, a person with a dual personality. But she preferred not to argue or discuss and instead left the place after humbly taking leave of Swamiji.

Back home, Radha thought over the events of the day. Her effort of finding peace of mind in the religious discourse had evaporated. She was back to square one. She got back to her routine but her mind was in constant turmoil. She had almost no one to talk to; no other hobby except reading. A visit of a relative was welcome. They would come and go. She spent quite lavishly, entertained them with good food but got tired after a few days. Prolonged stay of any guest was not to her liking. Perhaps this was true for all. At times she would get restless and lonely. On one such day, her aunt Sarla paid her a visit. She had come to the town for only a few hours but had painstakingly made it a point to call on her niece Radha and enquire about her welfare. Seeing Radha in such a depressed mood, she suggested Radha to come to her place for some time for a change. Radha found the suggestion appealing and for the first time in months went out of her home to live somewhere else. She found her aunt's company and hospitality a welcome change. After a week she came back home refreshed.

With this new experience, she made it a practice not to

ignore any invitation, even a casual one, and attended all family functions such as marriages, engagement ceremonies, *nam-karan* (Awarding name to the child), *ann prasana* (introduction of cereal food to a child) or even a death ceremony. Every such visit gave her new experiences, new acquaintances and in a way a new purpose to live. She was highly welcome on all such occasions because she was an asset; she was extremely well versed with all customs and rituals.

It was thus on this occasion of *ann prasana* of the daughter of Seth Dina Nath that Radha had graced the occasion with her visit and by her useful help in the proper conduct of the ceremony. The function of *ann prasana* finished smoothly and by next morning most of the relatives left except a few. Radha stayed on.

On the third day, Radha enquired about the horoscope of the child. "Yes," said Mr. Dina Nath." It has been duly prepared by a learned astrologer."

"Is everything alright?" enquired Radha.

"Well, there are some predictions which are gloomy," said Dina Nath.

Once again the horoscope was studied in detail. It predicted that the girl will have a tough time prior to her marriage negotiations and numerous hurdles will precede her marriage.

"Why not visit and consult Mr. Shastri?" said Radha. "He is reputed and endowed with divine powers and on meditation he can foresee events."

Dina Nath was averse to such consultation, but on persuasion he agreed to visit Mr. Shastri. The meeting was fixed for the next morning at 9 am They arrived in time, and waited for a while as Mr. Shastri was still engaged in *puja*. Finally they were all permitted into his chamber, where the floor was covered with thick mattresses and clean white bed-sheets were spread over the mattresses. Mr. Shastri was seated at the far end in quiet composure. He was a householder, a learned man, endowed with divine powers, and would not charge any fee or accept any presents. He lived a simple life and never boasted of his powers.

Seth Dina Nath and others removed their foot wears and entered the room and paid their homage to Mr. Shastri with folded hands. Mr. Shastri wished them back and requested them to be seated on the mattress. Radha introduced everybody and requested Mr. Shastri to enlighten them and help them with the matter of the child. On having completely understood the worry, Shastriji adjusted his seating posture, closed his eyes and went into a deep meditation. All remained seated in perfect silence. He remained so for about five minutes. Finally he opened his eyes and addressed Radha, "The girl is likely to lose her mother early in life. There will be heavy financial crisis for the family. She will have a miserable life before her marriage."

"Anything that can undo or mitigate the problems?" asked Radha.

"I am only stating the probabilities which I foresee. These may not happen at all," Shastriji said to console her. He then added, "Every trouble may be reduced to a large extent and sometimes can even be avoided by prayers, and by acts of charity and compassion to the poor and needy."

Seth Dina Nath looked somewhat relieved. But his apprehension continued and was very evident on his face. They thanked Mr. Shastri and left. Radha returned to her home after a few days, assuring Dina Nath that all will be well.

Time passed on, and as predicted, Pramela's mother expired suddenly after a brief illness when Pramela was only about six years old.

When Pramela reached high school, Kapil, the son of a

rich industrialist fried of Dina Nath, beacame a frequent visitor to her residence. He was tall, handsome and sophisticated. He owned several re-rolling mills. Pramela and Kapil used to converse for long hours, go for movies and often on family picnics. It was quite obvious that they would marry when of proper age. Kapil's parents had great liking for Pramela and they would have been glad to agree to this union. Meanwhile Kapil, after completing his engineering went to the United States for further studies leading to a post graduate degree in management. It was decided that he would return to India after two years and then will help his father in managing and further expanding the family business. Pramela and Seth Dina Nath were also happy for Kapil. Kapil completed his education in two years and did return to India but only for a week. He went back in spite of a lot of pressure to the contrary by one and all.

During the course of discussions with his father he stated, "There is no life in India, no dates, no outings, no get-together, no proper pubs or casinos or clubs. There is only dust and dirt, hypocrisy and corruption at all levels."

His father tried to argue but in vain, "Corruption is present in all countries." The father said, "It is all due to materialistic approach in life, lack of religious and human approach. It is only the quantum of corruption which varies."

"I agree, the corruption is prevalent in all the countries and is increasing," argued Kapil. "But it is the nature of corruption or the level at which corruption exists, that matters. In India corruption is rampant even at the lowest level; one has to struggle and waste time, money and effort and still suffer humiliations for routine work. Go to any government or semi-government organization and one is reduced to a level of a beggar. All are greedy, right from the peon to the chief secretary or a chairman!"

"I am afraid, you are a little too harsh on your own country, your mother land," said his father, Mr. Ramesh. "After all the country has been ruled by the British or for centuries and it is bound to petrify the moral of people."

"Have we really got the independence? Earlier we were ruled by British via their henchmen and today we are ruled by their petrified Indian version," said Kapil.

"You are hasty in your assessment. Anyways let us see what you propose to do in the United States for the next two years."

"I already have a good job secured for the next two years and then I propose to come back and settle here in India."

"Are you sure you are not going to extend your stay there indefinitely?" asked the father.

"I have no intention to do so as of today," said Kapil.

With this promise, Kapil went back to the States but at the end of the two years period, he got an excellent job with a much higher salary and challenging work. He could not resist the temptation and accepted the assignment for the next two years also. When this news reached his father, he was shocked and he assumed that his son would not return to India even after the next two years. He knew, people usually go on extending their stay in the United States, and subsequently get too accustomed to the life there that even a short stay in India would then be torturous for them.

Seth Dina Nath was equally perturbed. He was banking on Kapil for the marriage of Pramela. Pramela was now studying in college and had grown into an extremely attractive and poised girl.

# CHAPTER 2

Time passed, and Pramela got into the final year of college for her bachelor's degree. By this time, she had blossomed into an extremely beautiful and vivacious young girl. She almost always accompanied her father in the social meetings and functions. She also freely moved in the social circle of her friends, boys and girls of her own age and aptitude; and the same station in life. Hardly any evening passed when she remained at home. Her father, Seth Dina Nath, used to reach home from office usually late in the Evening, but always had dinner with her whenever both had no other engagement in the evening. Dinner time was one over which they would connect most, he would talk about his work in office, his business, about his friends and associates while she would talk about her studies, her colleagues and friends. And at the same time they would keep a required distance and talk with due regards with respect to the feelings of each other.

One bright October evening, when Pramela strolled through the decorated, beautiful lounge of Clark Hotel, people turned their heads to look at her. She was beautiful and had a perfect figure. A few continued to stare till she walked passed the entire corridor. Such was the spell cast by her dignified and cautious walk. A tall, well-built and extremely attractive man followed her and placed himself opposite her on a small table in a corner. His eyes held admiration for her bordering on infatuation.

"What will you have, dear?"

"As usual, a shot of bitter," she said. "It is quite hot for this time of the season. I feel frightfully thirty."

Vijay Singh, "Vicky" to his friends, ordered a drink, beer for Pramela and Gin and lemon for self, along with snacks.

Vicky pulled out a gold cigarette case from his pocket and lit a cigarette. Pramela was a non-smoker but she did no object to him or anyone else smoking.

Pramela wore a light make up that evening. In fact she at twenty one needed no cosmetics. She had dark black eyes, their shape resembling to those of a *ghazal* with beautiful thick eye lashes; black hair, straight from the top and curled at the ends. This combination, with her beautiful spotless skin made her devastatingly desirous. She had gotten accustomed to the praises of people of all age groups everywhere she went. It was thus natural that young boys of her age craved to seek her company, even for a few minutes. But she was completely devoted to Vicky.

Her father had brought her up to the best of his capability. She lacked nothing which a girl of her age and under her circumstances may desire; wardrobes full of beautiful, fashionable and expensive clothes, a car at her disposal, and enough money and freedom to enjoy the social life. She was in need of nothing and her mind was engaged largely in pursuit of social pleasure and this was nothing but natural.

Pramela did not know what scarcity was or how people of limited means managed to live. Most of her girlfriends were from rich families, the daughters of businessmen or industrialists or high placed officers with substantial incomes other than salary. On occasions when she found a girlfriend dressed somewhat modestly she would comment and apprise her of the latest in fashion. But she did not mean any insult, and her friends knew that about her. They took her remarks sportingly. In fact, she was very innocent, without any malice and unaccustomed to the life of bloating or cheating. Often, she was misconstrued as overbearing and pretentious by new acquaintances but her true simple nature soon dispelled these notions.

During a friends get together she met Vijay Singh and fell in love with him. She was so deeply influenced by his personality that she did not bother to find about his family background and financial status. To her, it was Vicky who mattered, and she dreamt of a happily married life with him.

Vicky was a man without a steady job and had a meagre income from the house in his ancestral town that was rented out. He lived with a divorced woman named Urmila. Though they were living together for sometime, yet he had not married her till now. She worked in a firm and earned a meagre salary too. Together they could manage a frugal life. But Vicky always wore good clothes and moved amongst the affluent society. Naturally he was always pressed for money and used to borrow from his friends and other associates.

Pramela was aware of Vicky's living arrangement with Urmila as he told her about everything at the beginning of the relationship. He thought that this would be the end of his friendship with Pramela but she was deeply influenced by him and also about his sincerity in telling about Urmila to her, that her love for Vicky got further reinforced. Vicky was eleven years older than Pramela and was an expert in flattery and intimacy. But she found him bewitching and they experienced great pleasure and thrill in this secret love affair, a secret from her father! Now, as Pramela was sitting in hotel Clark with Vicky opposite her, she suddenly felt uneasy. She was contemplating on her relation with Vicky and on their future. She wondered how long would she continue like this. Someday she would have to tell her father and seek his permission and blessings for her marriage. But she was vitally afraid of the impending causality. She knew it will be a difficult task. She asked Vicky, "How are we going to finalise the matter?"

Vicky paused for moment and remarked. "To my mind, there appears to be only one way out. We both must quit everything and go." Pramela mused, how lucky she was to have such a charming and sacrificing lover who was not at all interested in the fortunes of her family. But she was worried about her father who adored her, his only child.

"I do agree with you but for the mutual affection that I share with my father; which makes me think. He is old and with a heart problem. This would be too much for him to bear. Besides this, there is this concern about Urmila," said Pramela.

"Urmila will not be any problem," said Vicky. "She no longer loves me. Besides she is self-sufficient financially. I am sure she will not take it seriously, instead she would prefer her freedom."

"I am worried about my father," said Pramela. "It would be an unbearable blow to him, if we elope without his permission."

"He may forgive you in due course of time, but he obviously dislikes me and he cannot bear the idea of you marrying me. The news of elopement will be disastrous," said Vicky.

Pramela kept quiet, pondering deeply over the situation, but was unable to make up her mind.

She took a deep sigh and murmured, "It cannot go on like this too long. I desperately want to be with you forever for good or for bad."

"I wish there could be an easy way out," added Vicky.

"Also there is Tarun Pal," said Pramela. "Daddy likes him a lot, both for his humble and sophisticated nature and for his competence as a solicitor. Daddy has always wanted me to be nice to him."

The very mention of Tarun Pal, or Tony, irritated Vicky. He knew that Tony was in high esteem of Pramela's father and was a regular visitor at their residence. Seth Dina Nath simply adored him. Earlier Tony's father had been the solicitor of Seth Dina Nath. After his death, his son Tarun took over the charge. Now he was a friend. Seth Dina Nath wished that his daughter, Pramela pay more attention to Tony and be more friendly with him. But Pramela was bewitched by Vicky. The very mention of Tony made Vicky frown.

"You should be nice to him I agree," said Vicky. "But you don't love Tony, do you?"

"No, I like Tony, he is well mannered, nice and competent, but I definitely do not love him. I love you and you only."

On the spur of moment Vicky asked, "Would you have loved Tony if I had not come in your life?"

"I don't know. He is nice and good to talk to but I never had any feeling towards him other than that of a friend. You are simply amazing. Tony is just a good friend."

"Let us not bother ourselves with Tony," said Vicky. "Let us consider what we should do about ourselves."

"That is true. But I fail to find a solution," said Pramela.

He remained silent for a while, slowly sipping his drink.

Then Vicky asked, "Look here Pramela, why not precipitate the matter this evening?"

"What exactly do you mean?"

"Let us talk it over with your father this evening; tell him that we love each other and want to marry. I feel he will give the matter a favourable consideration. He loves you too much so he will not deny your ardent wish."

"I feel weak in such matters when I confront my father," said Pramela. "He grants me all my wishes, allows all expenses and all the freedom of movement. But in the matter of matrimonial alliance, he is still slightly conservative. The status of the family and the qualification and earning of the future bridegroom are very important to him."

"Let us give it a try, don't you love me enough to take up this matter and face the music? At least it will give him food for thought and he may relent in the near future," said Vicky.

"I love you too much to face any eventuality, but let us think over the approach first," said Pramela.

"Let us have dinner and discuss the matter," said Vicky.

"Yes, we should," she said.

"What would you like to have?" he asked.

"Anything light, no particular preference," she said.

"I will go and place order for something really special for you," he said.

He had a feeling that this dinner would be an important landmark in their future lives. He hurriedly left her and headed towards a man of his acquaintance whom he had spotted a few moments earlier at the bar.

Without wasting any time on preliminaries, Vicky straightaway asked, "Would you oblige me by a four hundred rupee note, buddy. I am broke and I have to buy my girlfriend dinner."

The man so approached was himself broke but he gave the sum to Vicky who soon returned to Pramela. Pramela was unaware of all this transaction. She still thought that Vicky was very well stationed in life and money was no problem.

Vicky returned to her and behaved the rest of the evening in a very polite and seductive manner. He was endowed with the faculty of smooth talking and at this juncture he was fully exploiting this faculty. Pramela was deeply impressed and convinced by Vicky. Ultimately she said, "Let us take the plunge this evening. I will talk to Daddy and I feel he will accede to our alliance."

"I pray to God; he does," said Vicky.

Vicky made the payment for dinner and they walked out of the hotel.

She stopped a passing taxi and the two proceeded for her home. Both were highly apprehensive regarding the outcome of their proposed meeting with her father. As the taxi entered the gate of the bungalow and approached the porch, the head gardener came running to them and gave the sad news that her father Seth Dina Nath had sustained a massive heart attack and was admitted in the medical college hospital. Pramela's heart skipped a beat.

"Oh Daddy," she moaned, her face turned pale and she felt as if she'll faint. Vicky put his arm around her waist to support her. Once she recovered from the shock she felt the urgent need of seeing her father. The taxi was still there. Pramela and Vicky again sat in the taxi and headed to the hospital, which was not too far. But to her time seemed to be crawling; she wanted to be at the hospital instantly. Now she realized how much she loved her father and how much dependent she was on him.

When they reached the corridor of the intensive 'Cardiac Care Unit' where her father was undergoing treatment, she enquired about her father. She was told that the condition of her father was very serious and nothing could be predicted at the moment. Tarun Pal was already there, overseeing all that needed to be done. Some of the close friends and relatives had been informed and they had gathered to wait in attendance too. Of course, no one could be of any further assistance. An hour passed, and Pramela advised Vicky to leave since a good number of people were already there and most importantly, Tarun was there to take care of things. He was playing the role of the son of the family. He also persuaded Vicky to go since everything had been taken care of and that he would be informed about the general condition periodically. Vicky was keen to leave but was outwardly reluctant fearing that Pramela may take it as his reluctance to help. Now on persuasion by both Pramela and Tarun, he left for home after extending a promise from Pramela that he will be kept informed.

As he left, all other people remained seated, waiting for some good news from the Doctor; for improvement in the condition of Seth Dina Nath. Tarun had missed the dinner as he had come rushing to the hospital after being informed of the situation. A few others had also not eaten anything since afternoon coffee. He, therefore, ordered from the hospital canteen; and coffee and some snacks arrived for all. Although no one was in a mental disposition to eat anything; Tarun insisted everyone to eat a bit at least.

It was about 10 pm when the doctor informed them that the condition of the Dina Nath was slightly better and only one or two people may see him for a brief interval of time but care was to be taken to avoid any emotional stress. It was decided that only Pramela and Tarun would see him. Pramela, on entering the room, found that her father looked very pale and weak. He opened his eyes and looked at her with fondness. A feeling of great affection filled her heart and she wished she could keep on looking at him for a long time. He tried to open his mouth to murmur a few words but Pramela forbade him from speaking as it would strain him. But she could not control herself for long and tears started dripping down her cheeks in-spite of all the effort she put in to not to do so. After a few moments her father beckoned her to come near. As she did so, he gradually lifted his hand and rested it on her head as if to bless her. He also called Tarun and blessed him. Pramela could not truly apprehend the significance of these gestures but felt happy at the same time. Soon thereafter the doctor bid them to retreat and permit the patient to rest. They came out and remained in the corridor.

A brief conference was held and it was decided that Pramela, Tarun and Ramu, an employee of the firm, would stay at the hospital while the rest would go home. Thus the three stationed themselves there for the night. Nothing could be done except to pray to God for Seth Dina Nath's quick recovery. Pramela dosed off after some time. It was about 4 a.m. that a nurse ran out of the ward and informed Pramela that her father had suffered another heart attack and that they were giving every medical aid that was needed. But half an hour later he was declared dead.

It was a massive shock to Pramela. Tarun was also deeply shocked since he had lost not only a valuable client but a father figure.

Pramela was so much in grief that she could not think of anything that needed to be done. Again, Tarun took the charge of the situation. He arranged for the dead body to be brought home, and informed all relatives and friends. Funeral was done on the bank of river Yamuna in the afternoon and was attended by vast number of relatives, friends and well-wisher. This was followed by thirteen days of mourning as was customary. All relative in other towns were duly informed and they arrived as was convenient to them. Radha was one to arrive the earliest. She took control of domestic affairs. Much was to be done during these thirteen days and finally on the thirteenth day final rites were to be performed. On the third day after the funeral, the ashes of the body were collected from the funeral pyre and were subsequently immersed in the holy river Ganges at Prayag, the confluence of rivers Ganges and Yamuna. The final rites were performed on thirteenth day as per Arya Samaj System; Vedic verses were recited, *havan* was performed and prayer was offered to give peace to the departed soul.

This interim period of thirteen days is usually a time of tension and turmoil. If the person has died without leaving a will and further more if the property is sizeable, several near and far relatives enter the arena of being claimants and everyone wants the maximum possible from it. Legal cases often get started. However in this case, everyone knew that not much would be left after paying all dues and debts. Accordingly the matter ended quite peacefully and everyone was apparently sorry for the sole survivor Pramela. She had to face the music soon after the death of her father. Tarun was the family solicitor and was a great help; in settling the financial matter and in handling family matters also.

Vicky was shocked at this turn of fortune. He had been looking forward to a life of luxury and relaxation on marrying Pramela, the only child of Seth Dina Nath. He cursed his fate but could do nothing. The family had little left now and his love for Pramela evaporated. However he maintained the pretence of deep sorrow and remained a daily visitor to her place.

Once the final rites were over, and Tarun came to Pramela's residence, she enquired,

"Tell me ever thing, where do I stand now?"

Tarun was apt in handling such cases and he had already worked out and found that Pramela would be left with almost nothing on settling all dues. But he thought it fit to reveal the truth gradually and accordingly he remarked,

"Your father had not been doing well financially for quite some time but now the position had been worse. I have still to work out the details." He did not give the full picture of the gloom nor did he give fake hopes.

Pramela was shocked to listen to Tarun but also realized with guilt that while she was wasting money in clubs and hotels, her father had been struggling for financial survival alone. He never let her have even a glimpse of impending crisis. Perhaps he felt that with some good stroke of fortune he would be able to overcome the crisis.

"I wish, I had known about it earlier," said Pramela.

"But you could have done nothing. It was perhaps all destined," said Tarun.

"Yes, I agree I could not have done anything. But at least I could have talked to him regarding the financial matters and could have given him moral strength. Perhaps he would not have taken it so seriously," she said.

"Perhaps you are right. But he did not want to bother you with his financial difficulties and he had forbidden me to tell you anything."

Tears braved to come out of her eyes and she said, "God, he suffered all agony by himself and even in his worst days he was careful not to bother me. How I hate having all the fun and spending lavishly while he was labouring under acute financial crisis."

"I pray, don't bother your precious little head on matters

which are gone and belong to the past. Nothing can be done now except to salvage what remains of his property and pay the debts," said Tarun.

Pramela raised her head and looked at Tarun. She found him so young and still so competent, confident and reliable. Although Tarun was a frequent visitor of her residence she had always looked upon him as someone drabbling in financial matters and as her father's equal in such matters. He hardly had time for clubs, bars and hotels. Such things, he thought, were for the relatively younger people. Serious matters concerning finance bored her and subconsciously she had developed an impression that a person deeply engaged in either earning money or its management or accounts were dull and drab; as machines for manipulating money. She had great regard for Tarun but had no tender feelings for him.

Now when in this hour of distress, she looked at Tarun with tearful eyes she was inclined to believe that he was handsome and a gentlemen. She was much infatuated by the smooth talk of Vicky that she had never really looked at Tarun. This was in-spite of her father's garbed hints to pay more attention to Tarun. But what was more important was the confidence and intelligence that radiated from him. But her fascination for Vicky completely overhauled all her tender feelings for Tarun. He was a family friend, a help and nice guy; that was all.

She remained quiet for a while and then asked Tarun, "Please tell me, where exactly do I stand financially now. Will I be penniless?"

He paused a few seconds but reluctantly said, "I am afraid, there may be nothing left worth minting. His liabilities are large."

"Will the house remain with me?" enquired Pramela.

"I am afraid, no; you may be permitted to keep the so called *streedhana* i.e. the ornaments and the jewellery exclusively belonging to the ladies of the family," said Tarun.

Pramela turned pale at the thought of impending financial inadequacy. Tarun looked at her small, tender self. His heart was pounding as it had never done before. "Pramela, my dear, have a heart, everything will be alright," he said to console her and boost her morale.

"Yes, I am sure everything will be all right. I must brave myself to the altered situation in life and pray to God to give me enough strength to even be happy in it," she said, having suddenly empowered by some hidden strength, the strength lying dormant amidst the luxurious life.

Tarun looked at her with appreciative eyes. He had seen her grow from early child hood and of late he had cherished a fond hope that someday she may belong to him. He was ten years older to her and thought that hardly mattered. He had an excellent practice and a high position in the society. Even Seth Dina Nath wished for Pramela to marry him. But he could never marry her against her wishes. When Vicky entered in the life of Pramela, the matter changed. He was endowed with the faculty of attracting any girl by his smooth talk, flattery and pretences. It was but natural that Pramela succumbed to his charm. Tarun on the other hand, was honest, upright and frank. At this moment he was doing all he could to help her and boost her morale.

But she was deeply in love with Vicky and was thinking of discussing matters with him at the earliest. Her father was dead now and hence there was no question of seeking his permission. She knew her father was against her marriage to Vicky. Under these conditions, she and Vicky could go ahead with the marriage. She knew that Vicky was not very well off financially but she could sacrifice everything for love.

She expected that Vicky would soon discuss with her their marriage plans.

Pramela had a faint idea that Tarun liked her and would be glad to marry her. But he had never proposed to her from the fear of getting turned down. He knew that she was madly in love with Vicky and she was confident that Vicky would seize this opportunity and marry her immediately.

Tarun was fully acquainted with the flirtations nature of Vicky, his poor financial position, lack of any steady job and about his unwed partner. He was saddened at the thought of Pramela marrying Vicky. But love is blind and she would not listen to Tarun's reasoning.

Never the less he tried to make a final attempt to talk to Pramela about marrying Vicky, entirely for her sake. He knew her life would be ruined if she would marry Vicky. He, therefore, took courage and spoke to her.

"Pramela, I pray you think very seriously before you marry Vicky. From all I have learnt, he is unsettled financially and far from deserving you as his wife."

"I have already decided. He is simply adorable. I am sure we will be very happy. We love each other deeply and that is what matters," said Pramela.

"What about the woman he is living with?"

Pramela felt a little irritated and said, "I feel deeply sorry for her. But I am sure Vicky will leave her and he says that she would not mind."

"I am afraid, she will create problems."

"Vicky has already spoken to her. Perhaps he will have to pay her some money."

"Does Vicky have enough money to cough up and also to support you maintaining the standard of living you are accustomed to?"

"I don't mind a lower standard. I can manage on much

less. Love gives you strength to enjoy under all circumstances," said Pramela a little philosophically.

Tarun felt disgusted. Pramela was not prepared to see the reality. He was afraid; she was far too young and immature to take a correct decision. However, under the current circumstances, he preferred not to interfere and let the future decide the matter.

"Pramela, I am not only your solicitor, I am your friend too and you can always bank on me for any advice or help if the necessity arises. I wish you all the happiness."

He paused for a moment and further added, "For the present, I will manage your family funds and once you two have settled down, I will leave the matters to you. But I again pray, never hesitate to contact me for any help, I repeat any help, that you may need any time."

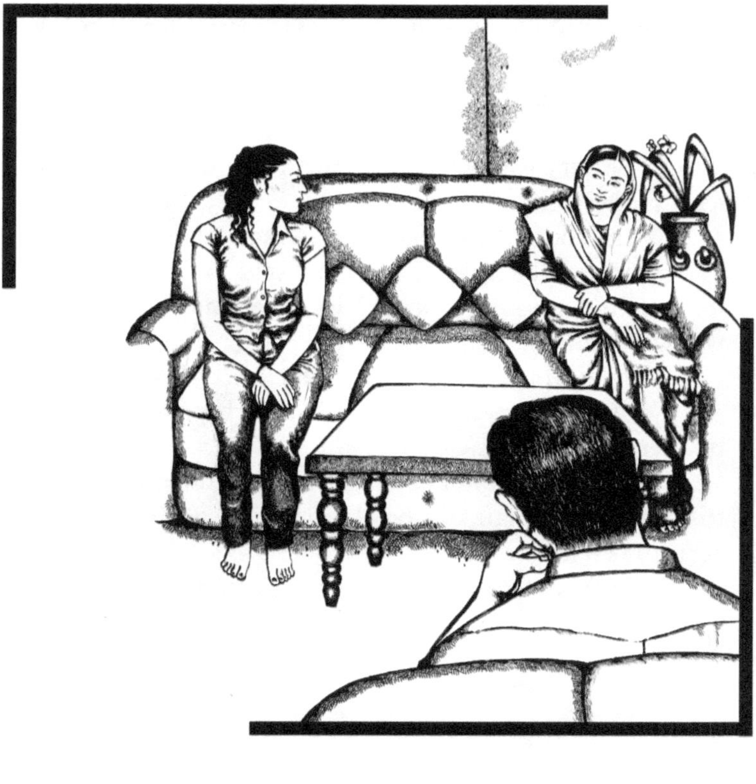

Pramela felt happy at what he said. Tears rushed to her eyes. Soon she regained her composure and said, "You are so helpful and considerate. I am so happy to have such a good friend and a well-wisher. I promise I will always remain in touch with you and pray for you to continue to be so benevolent after I and Vicky get married."

Tarun was a constant visitor to the house and remained with Pramela to attend to the routine domestic needs and also to the affairs of late Seth Dina Nath's estate. Most of the relatives who had come from other cities had left. Only her *bua* (aunty) Radha remained.

Most of the family continued to pay a visit occasionally or telephoned to sympathise with Pramela. Soon, however, the visits and calls started decreasing in numbers and frequency. One exception was Savvy, a close friend of Pramela, her own age and from relatively modest background. She was deeply devoted to Pramela. Most other friends simply vanished from her life. Even a few who were genuine friends of Pramela, could not afford time being engaged in their affairs and problems. Savvy was, however the exception. On learning about the sad and sudden demise of Pramela's father, she immediately packed her suitcase and shifted to Pramela's residence to stay with her so that Pramela may not sleep alone and also to provide her company.

Situation had indeed changed tremendously since the death of Seth Dina Nath. Considerable expenses were required to be incurred till the final rites. Her *bua* prepared a list of some grocery items to buy. Pramela asked Asha, the housekeeper to call their grocer, 'Modern Stores', where the family had an account. The dealer was quite rude to her and refused any delivery except on cash basis. Pramela was shocked. She had failed to appreciate the changed situation fully! The grocer was aware of the situation and was afraid that he would not get the payment for the goods delivered. This was only the beginning. Similar responses were received from all other parties.

This was definitely tough for Pramela and she was gradually appraised of her new situation in life. Every day now she learnt new lessons about the ways of the world. The very people who liked to invite her and spend lavishly on her, now preferred to avoid her. She had become a nonentity.

When Vicky came to meet her, she referred to the incidence and remarked, "How much have people changed now. Even the grocer is not prepared to give anything except on cash basis."

"What a shame!" he said quietly.

He knew quite well that she was broke now and therefore, she was not going to get anything on credit. He was moved by her misfortune and he saw that her eyes no longer held the spark which made her look so fascinating earlier. To console her he remarked, "It hurts me immensely to see you look so sad and dejected." She tried to smile but the true radiance of happiness eluded her eyes.

Vicky knew that he would have fully enjoyed the fortunes of Pramela had her father been alive and had Pramela married him. However, under the present condition, he was not prepared to share her pecuniary trouble. He was, however, very eloquent in his lip service. He therefore added, "It drives me crazy to see you so less now. I wish I could be here all the time to console you and to be of any assistance to you. I obviously feel envy of Tarun being always in the house here."

"You don't have to envy Tarun. He is our family solicitor and now Daddy's executor. Naturally he has to be here most of the time. I admit he is a great help in every possible way; I don't know what I would have done without him."

This statement further irritated Vicky and he said defensively, "Pramela, you really need the company of a friend to keep you in good humour. I wish I could have been here for more time."

"I agree with you. Whereas Tarun had looked after all the work that need be done, the real strength to face this calamity comes from you. You have been simply wonderful," said Pramela.

Time passed on. The final rites having been completed, Pramela had to pay more attention to winding up the affairs at home.

Vicky, as usual, came one morning to give Pramela a little company and to further enquire about her financial position.

He was deeply worried. If she stood to lose everything, then she was of no use to him. Yet he continued to keep the pretence.

"I don't know what is going to happen; Tarun said yesterday evening that my father had lost up to his last rupee. I shall be left with nothing but family ornaments and my personal clothes," said Pramela.

"How can they be so cruel?" casually remarked Vicky. His mind was busy wondering where he would stand financially if he married her.

"Tarun said that most of my friends would desert me once they become aware of my situation. *Bua* Radha corroborated it," continued Pramela.

Vicky again frowned and said somewhat irritated, "Tarun is an awful person; hardly can stand him. And your auntie Radha has gone senile."

But Pramela defended them by saying, "Tarun is highly competent in his work and is very cooperative, only he is straight forward and has somewhat a crude way of putting things. As far as *bua* is concerned, she is extremely useful and at a situation such as this, she is simply indispensable."

Suddenly Vicky asked her. "What is the reaction of Tarun regarding our marriage?"

"Well, he did not like it although he did not say so in words. You know, Tarun is like a family member and with Daddy no more with us; he is a sort of custodian of all family matters. He is obviously not happy with the idea of our marriage. But I am happy with the idea of our marriage."

"I know he does not like our friendship."

"I feel guilty, Vicky, I am snatching you from another woman. The only solace is that she does not care for you any more," said Pramela.

"Oh, don't worry your little head over her affairs. Let us

continue to be friends and enjoy life as it comes," said Vicky a little carefully.

"But I am all the while worried about the future. How soon can you get separation from Sarla, the women you are living with? You said earlier that she wants to leave you."

Vicky realized then that the matters were coming to a final showdown. He and Sarla had, of late, become extremely impolite to each other and when Vicky once dared to tell her to leave so that he may marry Pramela, she shouted.

"Don't be silly. We both are in heavy debts. If I can find a rich man, I will not hesitate to leave you. In fact, I had been banking on the money you would have inherited on marrying Pramela. But now the table has turned. She is broke. You would be a fool to marry her. Try and catch a rich woman. That is the only way out."

Vicky agreed with the logic put forth by Sarla. He therefore, thought to postpone his marriage with Pramela as much as possible and to find a way out. He had made up his mind now not to get involved in marriage with Pramela. In fact he felt as if cheated by Pramela because of this sudden death of her father. Money was the main consideration in his mind, but he preferred to avoid or at least postpone confrontation as much as possible. He accordingly said, "You perhaps do not know Sarla quite well. She will leave only if I pay all her debts and leave a lumpsum of money for her future adventures." The argument appealed to Pramela but she realized that such a situation was never told to her by Vicky before. In fact he had been pressing for their marriage at the earliest. Suddenly the death of her father had changed the situation. She reasoned that perhaps Vicky did not truly love her and was only after her money. But her heart was not prepared to accept it. May be that lady Sarla had shown her his true colours now.

However, Pramela loved Vicky so intensely that she was prepared to discount all his follies. However she swallowed her pride at this juncture and preferred not to press the matter further. She instead, accorded greater priority into preparing herself to the fare of all the eventualities that may arise as a consequence of the death of her father and her monetary inadequacy. She simply required some time to settle in her emotions.

"I wish I could part with the desired sum but under the present condition, I am not likely to have any substantial assets left after clearing all dues."

Pramela was now less bewildered and more self-confident than at the time of her father's death. She could now think straight and prepare herself for the worst. She seemed now to be possessed with considerable moral strength which had so far been lying hidden and untapped.

When Tarun came in the evening, Pramela insisted on discussing the financial matters.

"It is obvious now that I shall be left with nothing except my personal possessions and family jewels once the house is sold out," said Pramela.

"I am afraid, that shall be the position," said Tarun. "Of course the agricultural land may remain with you too."

"In that case I must leave the house as soon as possible."

"That is true. The longer you stay here now, greater the debt," said Tarun. "I will try my best to get as much as possible for the assets. If God wishes, you might be left with some money. But I don't want to give any false hope. It is only a wild guess."

"I have prepared myself mentally for all eventualities," Pramela said with firm determination.

"Have you and Vicky discussed the matter fully and come to some definite line of action?"

Pramela took a sip of coffee and said thoughtfully, "Yes, we have talked over the matter. We will marry as soon as he can get rid of Sarla." She hesitated to elaborate the matter further.

"But what is the hitch on the part of Vicky and Sarla. I thought they had come to some understanding, didn't they?"

"The situation has changed now. She demands money from Vicky to pay back her debts. Of course, Vicky can always refuse her since they are not married. But then that will be highly unpleasant and no one wants it."

"So you came back to square one. Sarla wants money, Vicky himself is in debt and you have no money to bail them out. Where does it leave you?" asked Tarun.

"I am afraid, it is not a pleasant situation, but I am sure Vicky will find some way out. He said that he is likely to get some money from the sale of his ancestral property of which he is one of the claimants."

Tarun felt greatly distressed and he looked at Pramela with deep sympathy.

"Tarun, please do not bother too much; I shall be alright."

"That is okay, you are old enough to take your own decisions. But please be careful and let me know what decision you take."

"Certainly, I will always keep you informed and look forward to your advice and help whenever I feel the need. I can depend on you Tarun, can't I ?" asked Pramela.

"It will be my pleasure to be of any use to you. Never hesitate to contact me for any help," said Tarun cheerfully.

"I will talk to Vicky and take a final decision. I will let you know what I and Vicky decide."

"Please do that, meanwhile the official receiver will look to the disposal of the commercial assets of your daddy."

"I know sooner or later I will have to leave the house.

As you said sooner I leave the better since that will cut most of the expenses associated with the running of the household," said Pramela.

"Where do you propose to shift? Of course, needless to say I can always accommodate you. You may shift after your marriage," said Tarun.

"You are a dear one and highly dependable. For the present, however, I propose to put up with my friend Savvy. She is staying with me here but she will go home today and talk to her parents about my staying with them for some time so that I may take my final examination and also finalize my future plans."

Tarun faced Pramela gravely, "Savvy sure is generous and your close friend. Her father Justice Goyal is also liberal and cooperative but he may not like Vicky once he knows about his background."

"He may not like Vicky visiting me at Savvy's residence but we may meet outside and discuss things. I am sure I can prevail Justice Goyal to grant me this concession," said Pramela gravely.

Pramela was sure of herself but Tarun knew about her innocent heart which was still not completely exposed to cruelties of life. Whereas she admired Tarun's confidence; Tarun, on the other hand, had vastly struggled in life to have such confidence and reach this high position at a relatively young age. He did not reply to her but simply looked at her with both admiration and pity.

Pramela continued, "I have a day or two to take care of these personal items; family photographs and a few other items of little value but of considerable emotion."

"Please that and also separate your jewellery, clothes and other personal belongings."

He paused for a few second and then said, "I must take

your leave; work at the office is piling up."

"I must thank you for all that you have done for me," said Pramela.

"Oh, forget about it. It is my pleasure to be of some use to you and the family," said Tarun. "By the way, if you do not have any specific program in mind, I would welcome your visit to my place. My mother and my cousin Suman would feel elated."

"It is so kind of you to invite me," said Pramela. "I am thankful to you for your personal visit on the occasion of final ritual on the thirteenth day after the funeral."

"My mother loves you dearly and will certainly feel happy if you visit us," said Tarun.

Pramela closed her eyes for a fraction of a second and emulated the vision of Tarun's house. She often used to go there when she was a child and when Tarun's father was alive. She liked Tarun's mother, Mrs. Anita Gupta, who was a charming and virtuous woman, but somewhat conservative in her ideas. She didn't quite appreciate the liberal conventions of youngsters. As a result, now when Pramela had grown up, it was difficult for her to be frank and be herself with her. There was a sort of cultural gap. Mrs. Gupta could not appreciate the extremely candid behaviour of grown up, college going boys and girls, their get together, going to bars and restaurants and their free movements. Further there was the basic difference in the economic level. She and her husband at the time of their marriage essentially belonged to the middle income group but had steadily moved up the economic ladder. Although the standard of living had improved tremendously, the basic principles of life couldn't change appreciably. Mrs. Gupta remained highly religious; she would go to the temple every day; give alms to beggars. They used to have religious gatherings and worship at their residence and people were invited to participate. After the death of her husband, she continued to live in the same manner, only that she now devoted more time to worship and meditation every day. But she was simple at heart and would not think of harming any one even when provoked. Nor was she unduly proud of the current high economic and social status of her only son, Tarun. Pramela would often visit her, talk to her for long hours but could never be at total ease as she was with the parents of her close friends, people of equivalent affluence and liberal modern culture. She had never bothered to think or argue in her mind, what is good or bad in her present cultural pursuit. She had been enjoying life to the fullest and now the death of her father and sudden financial downfall did completely change the situation. For once she realized how hollow her friendship and association with her so called friends was. As Tarun had very rightly said, none of her boy or girl friends were truly sympathetic to her and were not prepared to help her in any way. They just performed their routine duty of paying condolences and forget all about her. The group had lost one and that was all. A fresh one, from a nouveau-rich family would join the group. It was thus a passing phase. However to Pamela, it was all too tiring and a novel experience. She had, to some extent, started understanding life. Of her friends, Savvy was the only one and very close to her and was prepared to do anything to set her on the right track.

It was under this condition that Tarun offered her to come and see his mother and preferably stay with them. This was a gesture Pramela highly appreciated. But for the last several years another member Suman joined Tarun's family, she was a niece of Mrs. Gupta, distantly related, perhaps a third cousin, of her sister's nephew. She was no blood relation to Mrs. Gupta. Pramela had met Suman whenever she went to

Tarun's place but she never liked Suman and found her dull and boring. She was apt at house hold work and was a great help to Mrs. Gupta.

Pramela knew that Suman deeply loved Tarun and was always ready to please him in every possible way. It was assumed that Tarun will marry Suman someday but unfortunately he didn't feel the affection mutually. He liked Suman, her efficient way of handling matters, her help in the family and her deep concern for him but all this could not kindle a spark of love in him for her. He had in his heart, only brotherly feelings for her. He would, no doubt, take full care of her and personally looked at all her needs. Pramela thought of this as an unusual situation. But then it was likewise!

To further the argument, of his sincerity to offer Pramela a place, Tarun added, "Remember Pramela, you always have a room for yourself in my house. You are welcome whenever you want to come."

Pramela was deeply moved by his sincere concern for her. He was a real friend and a well-wisher. However she mustered courage and said, "Thanks a lot for your generous offer. I will always remember that and avail the same as the necessity may arise. However, at the present moment, I feel I will go to Savvy's or may be directly to Vicky."

Tarun felt a little sad but soon recovered his composure. He took leave of Pramela and proceeded for his residence with genuine concern for Pramela and extreme dislike bordering on hatred for Vicky. Never the less he envied Vicky, a good for nothing person except a smooth talker who had so completely won Pramela's heart.

It was a time of extreme pain for Pramela. She had sweet memories attached to her parental palatial house and to every piece of furniture, every plant in the garden, the sprawling thick and smooth lawn and almost every item. She had kept herself busy packing her personal belongings. She had decided to go and stay with Savvy. It was a difficult and painful process – the process of sorting out things, which item to pack, and which to leave. A few items needed to be destroyed. She wondered now, how items pile up in a house unless sorted out or disposed from time to time. Every item seemed necessary for future use. But now she had to act with firmness. She knew she was moving to the residence of Savvy and she must keep the packages to minimum. Further she was not very sure of her own future. At this juncture she again thought of Tarun. She was so sure of his generosity. She decided to leave at his residence such packages which were not of immediate use to her and take with her the bare minimum.

She called Savvy and requested her to help her in sorting out things and in packing the things in trunks and suitcases.

"I am lucky to have you here Savvy dear," said Pramela. "I never realized sorting out things and packing would be such a tiring job."

"I am afraid I am also not much good at such work," said Savvy, "However I will try my best and we shall soon complete the work."

"I acknowledge that we both have been spoilt by our parents and that we have seen only one side of the life," said Pramela.

"Oh cheer up Pramela, don't blame yourself too much. How unexpected is such a misfortune of not having both the father and the money. We learn from life as the time passes. I pray for you to take things in good stride and don't be too depressed."

But Pramela was in a depressed mood. With immense effort she fought back the tears tending to flow from her eyes. She looked at Savvy and said, "I shall be all right. Father used to say; adversity teaches you more than a lifetime of luxury. Even friends drop you like a hot potato."

She continued, "The Verma(s) have been close friends of Daddy and used to call us frequently. I have so far rung up Mrs. Verma three times and each time I was told that she was Out on some work. Obviously she and her husband prefer to avoid me. I have no right to complain. I wish I could enjoy the present circumstances and derive some pleasure from them."

"It is very brave of you Pramela. I wonder how you have suddenly become so philosophical. I wish you can take things with that spirit. You will no doubt, reach very high in life. However, let us for the present put our energy into sorting out matters and see what best can be done.

By the way when is Vicky coming? You must speak to him frankly and know what he wishes to do in the present circumstance."

"He is coming this evening and we will finalize our next steps. He is such a darling and a great asset."

"I wish something good comes out from your talk. I propose you finish this job and leave for my home this afternoon."

Pramela had also gone tired of all the hard work to which she was not accustomed. She yawned, and said, "It has been a new and very sobering experience for me doing this type of job at this hour of the day. I am sure it will come hard for me to get accustomed to such hardship in my near future. You know, Vicky is not well off financially and I will certainly be required to do many jobs which I am not accustomed to."

After lunch, Savvy left for her home. Pramela continued with her packing work. She was happy at the thought that Vicky would be coming in the evening and she could unburden her troubles on him. He will definitely find some way out.

It was tea time when Pramela received a call from Savvy.

"Something terrible has happened Pramela," Savvy said.

"I hope everybody is alright. Please do inform me all about it," said Pramela.

"You know, Mr. and Mrs. Grover are very good friends with my parents. Somehow they have learnt about your relations with Vicky. They told my parents that Vicky is a unreliable, good for nothing person and has no source of income. He lives on the charity of his friends and that currently he is living with a woman as unwed husband and wife."

"O My God, so where that does leave me?" asked Pramela.

"My father has very emphatically forbidden me to have

any further relation with you since it may tarnish my image also. I am so sorry but the situation has completely changed," said Savvy.

This was yet another shock to Pramela and upset her totally.

"You don't have to be sorry Savvy," cried Pramela. "It is not your fault and neither that of your parents. I appreciate their view point. After all they also have to think in terms of your marriage."

"It is so sporting of you dear not to take it otherwise. I wish my parents had not taken up the matter so seriously," said Savvy.

"It is all right Savvy. You will always be my best friend irrespective of the present predicament," said Pramela. "Perhaps things may improve once Vicky leaves that woman and marries me."

Pramela said all this more to console herself rather than Savvy. In fact she was deeply worried now and also frightened.

But she mustard all courage and prevailed on Savvy to not talk anymore for now to avoid further annoyance from her parents.

An hour later, Vicky arrived at Pramela's residence. This was for the last time. This hour, he reflected, which had been the destination of his ambition but now was to become a thing of the past.

Pramela was in her bedroom and she saw Vicky Approaching from the hallway. Her spirit was suddenly elated and she rushed down the stairs to welcome him, being sure that at last she'll find her final salvation.

Pramela looked beautiful in her full length dress. Vicky cursed the old man in his heart for not leaving behind any money thereby depriving Vicky of both the enchanting Pramela and the money which ultimately would have come to him. But all the same he greeted Pramela with great display of warmth and affection.

"My dear Pramela, my sweet one," he uttered.

Pramela got overwhelmed by this display of deep affection by Vicky and she rushed into his arms. Tears rushed to her eyes and this time she didn't resist herself from crying. However, soon she recovered her composure and said, "It is great of you to have come. I have been so listlessly looking for you. I get great strength from your presence."

"What have you been doing today?" asked Vicky.

"I wasn't doing anything special, except for sorting out things and packing. Savvy was with me to help me do it."

"What a blow for you, having suddenly lost all the money and property. I am hurt to the core of my heart for you," said Vicky to console her.

She looked up at Vicky with her lovely eyes, full of affection and warmth for him. She felt endowed with such strength on being with Vicky and she couldn't resist saying, "I have been feeling so miserable all day. But now you have come and it as all so different. I don't know what I would have done without you."

She then gradually moved out of his arms and took him to the sofa and sat next to him. She kept quiet for a few minutes and finally said, "My dear, I wish to unburden all my tensions on you. You are my strength."

"You can always depend on me, my sweet Pramela."

"I have so much to talk to you and we only have ourselves to decide about our future as my father is no more. I am afraid I feel so desolate without you," said Pramela.

"Shall we go out for a while? Fresh air will surely help your spirit."

"That is true," said Pramela. "But I would prefer to remain at home as we are alone now, we may discuss quite freely about our future plans. You know time is running out and I must leave this mansion at the earliest. My future course of action fully depends on our plan."

In a way Pramela felt relieved. Earlier her father was the main concern in her marriage with Vicky. She felt so sure now that Vicky would jump at this opportunity and settle everything. However, to her utter surprise, Vicky evaded the issue and said, "You are for the time being going to put up with Savvy. I may use this period to finalize our arrangement."

Her face fell and she said in a subdued tone. "That was the program till this afternoon. But now situation has altered and I am not going to her place."

"But why?" Vicky asked in an irritated tone.

Pramela told him the complete story and apprised him of the altered situation. She felt highly dejected while describing the situation.

"Savvy's father belongs to the old school of thought," she completed the narration. "He is afraid my stay at his residence will tarnish Savvy's image and it will cause problems in negotiating her marriage."

Vicky felt highly disturbed and nervous. He had no intention of marrying Pramela now who had become penniless. But at the same time, he wanted to continue enjoying her company for as long as possible before the final showdown. But now the situation had taken a turn to his disadvantage.

Pramela looked at the dejected face of Vicky and to cheer him up she moved close to him and said, "I really do not mind this altered situation, since I have you to look after me. Only this will hasten our marriage."

Vicky kept quiet. He did not know what to say. Obviously it occurred to Pramela that something was wrong. She had expected him to jump at the suggestion.

"What is the matter Vicky? Are you not happy at the thought of our early marriage? We have been looking forward to it expectedly all this while," said Pramela.

Vicky still did not look at her and simply said, "Nothing is the matter."

"Look into my eyes, darling, I want to see the flame of our

love and enjoy it."

Gradually he lifted his head, looked at her for a fraction of a second and whispered, "It is a tremendously awkward situation."

"Please elaborate," said Pramela nervously. "Is Urmila not prepared to leave you?"

"She certainly is prepared but for a consideration. At the moment I do not have money to pay her. I am expecting some money soon. Then I will be free to leave her and marry you."

Pramela's face fell on hearing this and she got upset. This was the last thing she had been fully banking on, Vicky. She loved him so dearly that she was prepared to sacrifice everything but as it was, neither she nor Vicky had any money to patch up the matter. However, she recovered her composure and said, "But Vicky, why should she demand any money? She is not your wife."

"True, legally she has no right to ask for it. But it is the nuisance value. She will create scenes and talk ill of both you and me in the society. I don't care much about me but I don't want your image to be tarnished," said Vicky.

She sensed that something was amiss. Perhaps Vicky was no longer interested in her and this question of money was only an excuse for not marrying. But her heart was not prepared to accept the fact. She in her mind wondered, how the question of money had come up suddenly. She wanted to get the things cleared up.

"But Vicky dear, all this talk about money never came up earlier. We were to marry as soon as we got permission of my father and Urmila was to leave you," said Pramela.

"My dear, there is no question of money between you and me. Only I have to pay her. Earlier she was prepared to leave me for a paltry sum but today, for reasons best known to her, she had inflated the sum. But please don't worry

I will manage somehow. Only that this may take some time," said Vicky.

Pramela then felt that there was more to it than what his word spelled. Perhaps he was no longer interested in her as she had no money after the death of her father. She tried her level best to throw this thought out of her mind. Vicky was dear and she was so much in love with him. However she gathered all the courage and asked the question straight away.

"Vicky, as my father has died and left me without any money, is it going to make any difference in our relation? You still love me, don't you?" she asked.

He did not look directly into her eyes and he was not mentally prepared to answer the question point blank. He made another effort to circumvent the issue.

"It is so difficult to explain all this to you, darling," he said. "There was no question of money earlier. I am afraid; we have to face the fact. Perhaps you know I have never been well off monetarily and I have no spare money to meet Urmila's demand. I am still expecting some money from my inheritance and it is all uncertain and in any case it will take time."

Pramela was shocked. All her plans were misfiring. She had been struggling all this while and now this was the latest and most severe blow to her. She was now almost certain; Vicky wanted to marry her only for money. But she wondered how she was so blind to the arrangement. She remembered with pain, occasional hints from Tarun regarding the poor reputation and past deeds of Vicky. But she had discounted all that. She was so deeply in love that she thought that Tarun was jealous of Vicky and hence the remarks. But now the picture was clear. She, therefore, decided to face this fresh calamity with fortitude and make her plans afresh. All of a sudden she felt an outburst of enormous courage in her tiny mind to face this ugly situation she was in.

'The worst is over', she thought. Then why not enjoy, derive some pleasure out of the acuity of the pain. A painful pleasure she was experiencing. She never knew that she was endowed with such a huge resource of courage and ability to face the worst situations.

She looked straight into Vicky's eyes with anger on her face that came effortlessly, subconsciously carrying the faintest of smile. She remembered her father who adored her, gave her full freedom of action, money as much as she desired and prevailed on her to enjoy life to the fullest. But at the same time he preached her to develop the faculty of enjoying the worst calamity, not simply facing it but enjoying it. He was a philosopher and an ardent follower of the 'Bhagwat Geeta'. His philosophy of enjoying life and being happy diffused from his simple saying, "Enjoy the sun, enjoy the rain… Enjoy the pleasure, enjoy the pain…"

Paradoxically he himself could not truly follow his own thinking and succumbed to the heavy mental pressure. Perhaps it was his old age and a very weak heart. But Pramela now had derived new strength from this thought and prepared herself to face all eventualities. She thus faced Vicky with firm resolve.

"So you mean Vicky darling that you would marry me only when you get the money that you are expecting from inheritance," asked Pramela.

"Unfortunately that is the situation," said Vicky feeling discomfort at the frank and pointed question from Pramela.

"Meanwhile, you will continue to live with Urmila and continue meeting me," said Pramela.

"I have no other option. I wish I had some money so that

I could leave Urmila."

"You mean, you were fully relying on my money?" asked Pramela.

"I am afraid; you are accusing me of such ulterior motives."

"Let us be frank Vicky," said Pramela, with a show of annoyance, "It is time we leave all the pretence and come to the bare truth. The truth is that when you wanted to meet my father asking for my hand, you were sure he would help us and with his money you could persuade Urmila to spare you and search for a greener pasture. You also wanted to lead a life of pleasure on his money, and do no work. Is that not true?"

"Look here my dear, I only..."

"No further beating around the bush Vicky," interrupted Pramela. "Answer me, yes or no."

He was taken aback by her forceful assertion. He had always seen her as a quiet, rather timid and manageable girl. He found his way out, "Well, you are right if you want to put it so bluntly," he said somewhat bitterly.

She smiled at him, further adding to his discomfort and said, "I see you now in your true colour and I am happy. I would have hated to have been married for my money. Now since I have no money, I am free from your manipulating attention."

Vicky started feeling more and more restless. He was completely surprised with Pramela's attitude and was not able to face Pramela who was all smiles now instead of feeling irritated and angry as was expected from her. Her behaviour puzzled him and he felt that he now was a subject of pity and ridicule instead of hate and annoyance. He felt small. This further offended him. He preferred to remain quiet.

"Tarun was right. He had already assessed your true

colours. Only I was a fool not to see it, being so infatuated by you."

"Please don't drag Tarun into this matter. You know I don't like him," said Vicky.

"Do you think it matters to me anymore as to what you like or dislike?" said Pramela in a rather tough tone.

"My dear, try to appreciate my position," said Vicky. "I assure you, may always rely on me. I still love you and will continue to do so irrespective of what your financial position is. I can ditch Urmila for your sake. I suggest we leave together for Bombay. I still have some money of my own and in near future I am likely to get a substantial sum in inheritance. Everything will be alright once I get the money."

Pramela left amused by his silly proposal, and said, "You mean, you will quietly leave Urmila, take me to Bombay and we shall live there in the same way as you are now living with Urmila?" said Pramela.

"My dear, let us take life as it comes," said Vicky, "Let us bother about the present only. Why worry about the future? We will manage somehow. Since we love each other, a little shortage of money will not matter."

Now Pramela looked at him with disgust.

"Perhaps you want me to have a week or two with you in Bombay and then leave me to the mercy of God."

"I realize your position Pramela. I never said I will leave you. We will find some way out."

"What do you take me for? I am no cheap girl like your Urmila without any self-respect. I would rather live on pittance than accept your proposal."

"My dear, be broad minded. Try to enjoy life as long as it goes good. Why bother about the future."

Pramela suddenly trembled at the audacity of his proposal. She could no longer contain herself and burst out,

"Get out of my house Vicky and never dare to contact me."

Vicky looked at her angry face and realized that the matter was over. He had already realized what was in offing and had made a last minute effort to reduce her into his unholy proposal. He also realized how enchanting she looked when angry and cursed the God for the financial catastrophe and untimely death of her father. How wonderful would the life have been if he had survived and accepted the proposal of their marriage? But that was not destined and all his plans had failed. He realized the futility of any further persuasion. He accordingly gave one last look at her, and left.

Pramela once again assessed her situation. Her father was gone, Savvy's father would not accept her in his house, and Vicky had shown his true colours. Obviously she had to find some way out for herself. Of course, there was the offer of Tarun to come and stay at his residence. He was such a dear friend and helpful. But some thought dissuaded her from accepting the offer. She thought of taking up some job. But before that she must complete her exams to obtain her degree. This would entail a little over one month's stay somewhere. She knew that she would not be able to concentrate much on studies. But it would be better to take the exam and get the degree rather than leave at this stage.

She pondered on various possibilities. However, reverie was interrupted by the arrival of Tarun looking sober and confident as usual. For the first time, she closely looked at him and compared him to Vicky. He was no doubt handsome, well built, competent, honest and very well placed in life. In spite of this she could not harbour any feelings of love for him; she had all this while considered him only as the solicitor and a friend of the family. He no doubt, lacked the dash and smooth flirting habit of Vicky. But all the same she realized how happy would be the girl who married him. Her thoughts were broken by the greetings offered by him.

"You look so pale and run down; something serious? Please share it with me," Tarun said.

Pramela told him all about Savvy's father and about Vicky. She was obviously unwelcome at Savvy's place.

"I am now looking for a place to live for about a month to complete my studies and examination, only after that I may decide my future plan of action," said Pramela a little sadly.

"As I told you earlier, you are most welcome to stay at my house, I will feel honoured," said Tarun.

She was filled with a feeling of gratitude for him and was overwhelmed with his gesture. But she knew she could not avail it. She must be on her own. She felt it was difficult to decline this renewed offer without offending him.

"I am so grateful to you but I must not burden you with my problems. Already you have done so much for me. However if you can arrange some small and cheap but independent accommodation for me, it would serve my purpose for the time being."

"If you insist on not living in my house, I suggest you shift to the college hostel."

"I would love to do that but I am afraid, there is no vacancy," said Pramela dejectedly.

"If you permit me, I may try for you. I have some resources that may come handy."

Pramela was a little surprised. She had never thought of Tarun as anyone but a mere solicitor all the time busy in monotonous work. But she was glad at the same time and requested him to get her accommodation in the college hostel. Tarun also felt happy as he got an opportunity to be of some use to her at this critical juncture. He left with promise to see her the next day with some good news.

Once she was alone, she again got into a pensive mood, wondering how her situation has changed so radically in this short span of time. She felt so lonely and depressed. But the very thought of shifting to the hostel gave her some consolation. Her auntie Radha staying with her was a great help and a comfortable company. But the thought of facing life without money and any support disturbed her all the while.

Radha, as was expected of her, had offered Pramela to come and stay with her as long as she wanted. But her mind did not permit her to accept the offer, at least not for now. Radha was quick to read her mind and she suggested that Pramela should forget everything and concentrate on her studies. Subsequently she may decide what to do. Radha was worldly wise and had great faith in God. She said to Pramela, "Have faith in God. When one door closes, other door opens. There is always some way out."

They retired for the night. The next morning she kept herself busy in further packing but now she was not sure what she could do with the packages. By afternoon she looked forward anxiously for the arrival of Tarun. In her whole life so far, she had never been so eager to meet him. A sort of tender feeling was gradually sprouting in her heart for him. For once she realized how dependable, honest and helpful he was.

It was rather late in the evening when finally, Tarun arrived. Pramela received him anxiously and looked forward for the news regarding her accommodation in hostel. Tarun, however, informed her that he could not succeed in getting hostel accommodation for her as there was no vacancy at all. However, he could arrange for her stay in the working women's hostel.

"It would be a little costly," he said. "But more comfortable and free from disturbance permitting you to concentrate on your studies."

"Many many thanks," said Pramela excitedly. "When can I shift there?"

"Anytime you desire. I have completed all the formalities needed. However, officially, you are employee of my office and on leave for completing the examination."

Pramela was delighted but thought how things had changed. She was required to be shown as an employee in the office of her father's solicitor. Never the less she was happy that she would be on her own.

All the three, Pramela, Tarun and aunt Radha, sat in the drawing room and discussed the matter. It was decided that Pramela would shift to the hostel next morning with her books etc. and minimum luggage, while the rest of the packages would be sent to Tarun's place. Radha would also leave the same day. The house would be closed and Tarun would look into the financial affairs. Both Radha and Tarun offered to accommodate her in their residences after she got free from the exams. Further studies were obviously out of question.

Next morning Tarun came as was decided, packed her luggage and took her to the working women's hostel, met the superintendent Mrs. Prasad and settled her in her room. He personally surprised Pramela with the arrangement of furniture, books etc. and took her leave after everything was reasonably well in control.

"I will visit you after a few days to see if you need anything," he said.

"It is so nice of you Tarun," whispered Pramela with wet eyes. She was barely able to restrain her tears and felt sorry when he left. She lied down silently on her bed and pondered over the shift of fate and sad occurrences during this fortnight. It was indeed difficult for her to fully reconcile to her new situation in life. She also realized with a little surprise that she was developing tender feelings for Tarun, no longer was he just a solicitor of the family but a close friend, or was he now something more than a friend. With an effort she removed all the thoughts from her mind as she had to concentrate on her studies and then to plan her future life.

Time passed and Pramela kept herself fully engrossed in her studies. Tarun visited her periodically to enquire about her welfare. Once the exams were over, she felt greatly relieved and was now ready to face her future. She still had some money left in her personal account in the bank after paying all her expenses. But that won't last long, she knew. She had to learn to earn her living. With regret she realized that she had no specific training for any job. But this last two months had hardened her from the pampered daughter of a billionaire to a down-to-earth penny girl, one packed to the brim with self-confidence and enthusiasm. She had decided to try her hands on any job that came her way with strong determination. Packed with firm determination she decided to meet Tarun before taking the final plunge.

At half past three, for the first time in her life Pramela walked into the office of Gupta and Gupta, solicitors and chartered accountants. She had various matters in her mind she wanted to discuss – the current financial status of her father's property, possibility of her starting a humble business, possibility of her finding a suitable job.

As she entered Tarun's chamber, she saw him seated on an exquisite executive chair facing the door. The office was imposing, furnished with costly tables and chairs, thick wall-to-wall carpet and paintings of celebrities on the wall. The large teak wood desk, stacked with papers, added grandeur to the office. A large book case lined the walls.

As soon as she entered the office, Tarun got up and held out his hand, "What a pleasant surprise, Pramela," he echoed.

"This is your maiden visit to my office. Please be seated."

Pleasure was plainly smeared on his face.

"You look very composed and enchanting," he blurted out but realized immediately that the remark may be misconstrued by Pramela.

However to cover up the slip he continued, "It is indeed a pleasure to see you in good spirit after all that you have gone through recently."

"Thanks for the compliment," said Pramela, "Today I have come to discuss a very specific purpose."

"Please tell me. It will be my pleasure to be of use to you."

"Perhaps you are aware that my exams are over. There is no question of pursuing further studies," said Pramela laughingly. "I am here to seek your advice on my future course of action."

Tarun had a fleeting thought that perhaps she was talking about her marriage but soon he realized his mistake and ventured, "If you are not pursuing studies further, then you may take up some job or some vocational training."

"I have precisely the same thought in my mind, but I am not trained for any specialized job and going in for any professional training, would be time consuming and costly. I can hardly spend money on that."

"I may suggest that you take a job which does not require any specific training, get consistent with the job and then you may move on to a better job."

"Yes I will do that."

"But do take care of yourself and keep me posted."

"You are a really dear one Tarun," she said without hesitation. "I don't know what I would have done without you."

She left Tarun's office and returned to the hostel. She knew she could not continue for long in the hostel and must get a job so as to properly qualify to stay in the hostel. As her personal account was draining out; she knew, soon she would be left with nothing.

# CHAPTER 3

Pramela started to hunt for a job in right earnest. When her father was alive she used to travel either by car or taxi. But now she had to accustom herself for journey by bus. She now walked to the bus stop, waited for the bus to arrive and many times ran to catch the bus. Buses were usually overloaded and often she had to travel standing. It was all a new experience for her and now she realized what the life of a daily commuter was. Heat and dust made her perspire and feel greatly uneasy. But gradually she tried to get accustomed to it. When she returned to the hostel in the afternoon; she found herself fully exhausted and de-spirited. She would many times lie down and contemplate on her present state. This was the life of middle class people in the country. But she found that people were so accustomed to it that they enjoyed the bus journey with its jerks and jolts, heat and dust and often quarrels for getting a seat. People travelling daily in the bus were acquainted with each other and to pass time they would crack jokes, laugh and sometimes even make vulgar remarks. People next to such people never felt offended as well. There were seats reserved for ladies but most of them were always occupied.

Time passed and she realized that getting a job was perhaps the most difficult thing in the world. And the difficulty was compounded when one did not possess any specific skill in the trade. She realized the fatality of her education, an education that could not provide a job.

Half of the month passed in this possess of job hunting with no success. One afternoon on her return from her usual travel, when she entered her room she found two letters awaiting her attention. One was from her close friend Savvy. Her family had gone to their Dehradun house for stay during summer. Savvy had written this letter in her usual affectionate way, full of concern for her welfare which touched her deeply. She realized that she had at least one true friend who sympathized with her and would have done anything possible within her means. Tears trickled down her face when she had completed reading the letter.

The second letter was from her aunt Radha who had earnestly persuaded her to come and stay with her for at least a month to sooth her jarred nerves. This letter was in reply to one that she had written to Radha about her present abode and about her search for job. Pramela was moved by the sincerity of the offer and pondered over it. As it was she had no job and there was no certainty of getting one in the near future. Further her accommodation in the hostel had been arranged on compensation grounds and was for a limited period. She would be required to vacate the room soon. Considering all these facts, she decided to take a break and visit aunt Radha.

Once she decided to go to Radha's place at Kanpur she acted on it without further delay. She rang up Tarun to inform him about her program. Tarun was not sure how she would be received at Radha's place and how comfortable she would be. He was honestly concerned about her but he preferred not to dissuade her. He, however, took a promise that she would continuously keep in contact with him and that she could always depend of him. He once again told her that the doors of his home were always open for her and it would be his pleasure to accommodate her. She felt happy about the repeated offer but all the same she wanted to not accept it at this time. Besides, she was a girl of very high self-respect and wouldn't like to burden him unnecessarily. He was greatly obliging her already by managing the finances of the residual property of her father.

She made payments of all the hostel dues and took the train to Kanpur. To save money, she preferred to travel in second class coach, although during the lifetime of her father she always travelled either in first class or air-conditioned coach. She realized that she had to take economy at every stage.

On reaching the residence of auntie Radha, she found her expectantly waiting for her.

"I would have come to the station to receive you my dear had I known your program," said Radha.

"There is hardly any need for that auntie. I am no longer a kid and I can take care of myself," said Pramela, feeling happy at the benevolent gesture. "How is your health now?"

"Old age is a disease by itself. But otherwise I am quite fit except for my high blood pressure."

"Do take care and keep taking medicines regularly to control the blood pressure," said Pramela.

"I am told, meditation also help in such cases."

"You are right. I have learnt to meditate. It may be useful in controlling the blood pressure and in addition I get my peace of mind and that is what matters," said Radha.

"I hope I will not be disturbing your daily schedule. I will try to be least cumbersome to you," said Pramela a little apologetically.

"On the contrary, you will be a pleasure and an asset to me," said Radha.

"I am eager to know what all you have been doing since I left your house. But I will prefer you freshen up first. It is so hot and dusty in this season. You better take a bath and we will talk over a cup of tea."

Pramela indeed was profusely perspiring and badly needed a bath. She proceeded to the bath room and on return found Radha ready with tea and some snacks.

Tea liqueur was simple, not decanted from the connoisseur Darjeeling leaves, and was good all the same. Pramela prepared her own tea adding fresh milk and a teaspoon of sugar. Radha, on the other hand, added no sugar to her cup of tea, on doctor's advice. Her blood sugar was on the higher side and hence the restriction. Pramela enjoyed her cup of tea after the long and tiring journey in the crowded second class compartment of the train.

After Pramela recollected all the memories that had happened in the intervening period; about the offer of Tarun to stay in his home, about his arranging for her stay in working women's hostel, about her studies and examination and her fruitless efforts in getting a job; subconsciously she had praised Tarun for all his efforts of helping her and the sympathy. Radha had a sharp mind in assessing people, and she was quick to offer her comments concerning Tarun.

"Tarun is a gem of a person. He will make an excellent match for you," said Radha. "Even your father did place him in high esteem and had always wanted you to marry him."

"Oh auntie, you have turned into a match-maker," said Pramela laughingly, "I will marry a man I love. I too have high regard for Tarun but my heart does beat for him."

"I am not opposed to marrying for love but for successful marriage you must first love to your heart's content and must also differentiate between true love and a simple infatuation," Said Radha.

"I truly loved Vicky, it was not a just an infatuation and I would have married him if this incident wouldn't have happened," said Pramela.

"My dear Pramela, it was a one-sided affair. You loved Vicky deeply but he was simply a money hunter and a cheat; absolutely incapable of truly loving anyone. Your father and

Tarun could see through the fraud, but you were so blindly in love with him and hence didn't see his true colours."

"I must admit I couldn't judge him properly. But God has been great to save me, although at a very heavy cost, life of my dear father and ruin of family fortune," said Pramela repentantly.

"It is good you realized your mistake and I can assure you my dear you will be extremely happy if you marry Tarun."

"But how can I do that when I don't love him and even don't know whether he loves me or not," said Pramela.

"One thing I can assure you, Tarun worships the place where you put your feet. I have seen that in his eyes. He simply adores you but is afraid of expressing his feelings fearing that you may reject him. I am absolutely confident that you will be extremely happy on marrying him and you will, mark my words, start loving him."

"Aunt Radha, do you mean that marriage is a pre-requisite for love."

"I did not say that Pramela. Love marriage may be and are often quite successful. But it does not simply imply liking each other; it is much deeper than that, it involves care for each other, deep understanding with each other and finally sacrificing for each other. True love consists of all these factors and this is possible only after marriage."

"You may be right bua but at this moment I am not mentally prepared for marriage." said Pramela. "Allow me some time to get over all that has happened in the near past."

The discussion ended for the time being. Pramela enjoyed her stay with Radha. She started participating in house hold work. All this was a new experience to her. When her father was alive, as was customary in well placed families of industrialists and other rich people, all domestic work was done by servants, sometimes by as many as eight or ten per household. The lady of the house simply gave orders and managed things. Pramela also became quite apt in household management. The monthly provision and regular requirement of fresh vegetables and fruits etc. were ordered and stocked. The cook, his assistant and the buttler used to ensure preparation and service of morning tea, breakfast, lunch, afternoon tea and dinner. Visitors were similarly served proper food and eatables. Other servants included *malies* (gardeners), car driver, general attendants, those engaged in sweeping and cleaning the house, in washing and ironing the clothes and *durban* (gate keeper). It was a sizeable task managed by this force of servants and ensuring that everything proceeded properly.

Now at Radha's residence the general pattern was the same as in middle class families. Thus there were part time servants to sweep and clean the house, to wash clothes, to wash utensils and an attendant for general duties. He used to assist in shopping, purchase of vegetables and fruits, and help in cooking. Radha used to do her own cooking but was assisted by this servant, a boy, named Ramu. He would keep cleaning and dressing the vegetable, kneading the flour, soaking rice and pulses. Radha would put the pressure on the gas stove, cook lentils and prepare chapaties. Some times chapaties were replaced by *parathas* prepared with *desi ghee* (melted and purified butter that has been heated for a long time). Pramela now assisted Radha in cooking and soon became quite apt in cooking. Often she would accompany Radha for shopping. Pramela learnt all that she could from Radha and enjoyed it.

Although Pramela was quite happy and busy at Radha's place, she had a vacuum within her and also felt that she was wasting her time and failing in her duty in some way. She was dependent on Radha. Once she dared to talk about this and tried to compensate monetarily for her stay but Radha gave her much scolding that she dared not broach the subject again. But restless Pramela remained. This, however, was interrupted by a letter she received from Tara, who was the governess and sort of house hold supervisor when she was young. Before working for Seth Dina Nath, Tara was from a good family and was moderately educated but the sudden death of her husband at a relatively young age had left her destitute. She was happy when she found this job and shelter at the residence of Seth Dina Nath. Pramela loved her deeply and all the servants in the house too took orders from her but at the same time loved her.

The letter was in response to one Pramela had written to

Tara, explaining her position and seeking her help to get a job so that she could live on her own.

Pramela read and re-read the letter with deep affection. Tara had moved to her native town Jabalpur situated on the bank of holy river Narmada. Tara in her letter had urged Pramela to come to live with her as her honourable guest. Of course, job could be arranged for her. Pramela immediately made up her mind to leave for Jabalpur. Radha, of course, requested her to continue to live with her. "My current income is sufficient to support us both," said Radha. "There is no need for you to leave. Further you are an asset to me in running the house."

Pramela was moved by the affection showered by Radha. But she had made up her mind to be on her own. Her sense of self-respect was too powerful to avail courtesies of Radha any further. And there was a job opportunity offered by Tara. With tearful eyes she said to Radha, "Dear auntie I shall forever remain indebted to you for your affection and support given to me at a time when I needed it most. I have fully enjoyed my stay here but I no longer want to be a burden on you."

"You are not a burden dear Pramela, and would never be so. This is your home. Perhaps you cannot fully appreciate the timely help given to me by your respected father. When my husband died and all my relatives were after my property and money. But if not for your father, I would have been on the road. So my dear, never harbour the feeling that you are a burden on me," said Radha with tears in her eyes.

"Dear aunt, I am so grateful to you for your affection and kind words. I promise I will keep visiting you but at the present moment I need to go to Tara and take up a job," said Pramela. "Further I shall always remain in touch with you."

Radha, with a sad heart, agreed to let her go. Pramela wasted no more time. She packed her suitcase to leave by the afternoon train and reach Jabalpur the next day. But before that she dropped a letter to Tarun informing about her program and giving the address of Tara at Jabalpur. She also arranged for reservation in the second class sleeper bogie of the train. There was a separate compartment exclusively for ladies and it had six births.

She left for the railway station a little early to not let room for any possible delay due to road traffic. As a result she reached the station half an hour before the departure time. The train ran between Lucknow and Jabalpur. Lucknow was the first station. When she arrived at the station, the train was still in the yard and was due to arrive in fifteen minutes time. Pramela preferred to wait on the platform rather than going to the ladies waiting room. She found a seat on a bench on the platform and waited for the train to arrive. But the unkind fate brought her in contact with the one person whom she wanted to avoid the most. While surveying the platform through her eyes, her glance rested on a tall, well-built man standing at a distance from her, a figure all too familiar, dressed in beautiful cream safari suit and well-polished tan shoes. He was Vicky, carrying an expensive suitcase and presumably travelling by the same train.

For a tiny instant, Pramela's heart seemed to cease beating and blood rose to her beautiful checks. "Why should he be here?" she pondered. She wished that he missed seeing her or at least not travel in the same bogie. But her wish did not materialize. Vicky saw her; he approached her and uttered an explanation.

"Pramela, it's a pleasant surprise! You could knock me down with a feather. By the way where are you going? Jabalpur...?"

"Yes," she simply said.

"But, my dear, what a luck running into you like this,"

said Vicky. “I am also going to Jabalpur, but on the way, I will take a break at Katni and visit the famous Bandargarh National Park. It is a beautiful place which abounds with wild animals like tigers, leopards, panthers, bears, and of course, deer, monkeys, etc. An elephant ride is exalting. I suggest you come along with me and later I will drop you at Jabalpur.”

It was uppermost in her mind to avoid him at any cost. So she simply said, “Thanks for your offer. But I am going straight to Jabalpur and my program is fixed."

"But why are going to Jabalpur?" he asked.

"That is hardly your business," said Pramela, a little irritated.

"Are you travelling all alone?"

"I don't see that it should concern you," she said to close the undesired conversation.

He gave a subdued laugh and shook his shoulders.

"Can we be friends for old time's sake?"

Pramela gave him an indignant look.

"You obviously have no sense of shame, talking like this after what all happened?"

"What should I be ashamed of…?"

"No, perhaps you don't feel the necessity. I now see your very true colours. You, with your poor cultural and intellectual breeding won't feel ashamed after the way you behaved…?"

"Oh, dash it all. Why call names. Life is to enjoy. Enjoy it while it goes good. I see no harm in it."

"That is what you think. I don't subscribe to it. I refuse to discuss the matter further and pray you leave me alone."

"My dear, don't be stupid," he said in a quiet tone,

"There is no need to be fussy about things. We are both going to the same place, both have same stupid luck and I see no reason why we cannot be friends, enjoy life and if need be, part company and travel our own ways."

Pramela got highly agitated. This was something she never expected of Vicky. With great effort she controlled her anger and said,

"Look here, Mr. Vijay Singh. Enough is enough. I have no money no doubt but I am still the daughter of my father who was a multi millionaire and philanthropist. I have inherited the essential culture of the family although I have been mixing freely in society. Our culture does not approve free sex, if that is what you have degraded yourself to. I am soon going to enter my train compartment and pray to God never to come across you in future."

Vicky was slightly disturbed by this sudden outburst of annoyance. Vicky wanted to continue his talk but the train slowly crawled on to the platform. Pramela lifted her suitcase and started towards her bogie but stopped as she saw someone running towards her with a briefcase in hand. Her eyes widened with astonishment as he saw Tarun approaching; yet another surprise for her. Vicky also saw Tarun coming their way and guessed perhaps Pramela knew he was boarding the same train. He inferred that it was because of Tarun, Pramela had snubbed him so roughly.

In the spur of the moment, Vicky moved away to a position where he could not be seen.

Tarun, in the process of managing the assets of late Dina Nath, needed Pramela's signatures on certain papers. He thought of writing to her at her Lucknow address. But meanwhile he found the need to travel from Delhi to Lucknow to see an old and valued client, an old lady named Mrs. Anuradha Sharma. He discusses the financial matters with Mrs. Sharma for about an hour and had tea with her. Mrs. Anuradha Sharma, who knew Seth Dina Nath and about his sad and sudden death, enquired about her daughter: "It is so unfortunate for that poor girl," she said to Tarun. "Where is she now?"

Tarun told her all about Pramela, about her current poor financial position and about her currently stay with her aunt Radha. Mrs. Sharma was a widow with considerable wealth and respectable position in the society. She was deeply concerned by the sudden calamity befalling on the daughter of Seth Dina Nath and she said to Tarun,

"I would very much like to help the girl . But at the outset I would like to meet her. If she has no objection, she may stay with me for a few weeks. It would be useful to her strained veins. Please if you may contact her and convey my interest in helping her."

Tarun was well aware of the independent spirit and high sense of self respect in Pramela. He was not sure whether Pramela would accept the offer made by Mrs. Sharma. He, however, promised that he will contact Pramela and request her on behalf of Mrs. Sharma to join them for dinner at the residence of Mrs. Sharma.

The old lady was delighted and looked forward to meeting Pramela in the evening.

Tarun accordingly went to the residence of Radha and was told that Pramela had just left for the railway station to take the afternoon train to Jabalpur. This was something unexpected. He loved Pramela from the bottom of his heart and got worried. He immediately rushed to the railway station with the hope to find if she may be interested to meet Mrs. Sharma and talk to her. And he was lucky that day. He saw Pramela on the platform. His heart gave a sudden and brisk jump.He saw her preparing to broad the train. He was delighted to see the charming face of Pramela. But he also saw to his surprise a tall man standing at a slight distance from her, Vicky.

Tarun was taken aback. He jumped to the conclusion that they were going together and this had accounted for the sudden departure of Pramela. His heart twisted and his throat got dry. However he controled his emotions. He still considered himself in the triple role of a guardian, a protector and a friend to Pramela. He made an extreme effort not to lose his calm.

He quickly approached Pramela.

"Tarun, what a pleasant surprise, seeing you at this moment," uttered Pramela with great delight.

Tarun did not fail to see the real pleasure on her face but he was intrigued by the presence of Vicky.

"Where are you going?" he asked in a somewhat hoarse tone. "Why are you doing this?"

It was now Pramela's turn to be surprised by this undue outburst.

She stared at him but calmly replied, "I am going to Jabalpur."

"You have broken your promise," Tarun said, feeling jealous because to the presence of Vicky. Meanwhile Vicky had moved away so as to avoid any confrontation.

"What on earth do you mean? Why are you so perturbed?" asked Pramela.

"You gave me your solemn promise to have nothing to do with Vicky. But now I find you two going together to Jabalpur. I am greatly disturbed by your behaviour."

Pramela took a second to grasp the full significance of this accusation. She smiled and said,

"Just a moment Tarun, please be good enough to explain. What made you think I was going to Jabalpur along with Vicky?"

"He is here with his luggage, all set and ready to board the train," he said with a somewhat hot tone. "You can't deny you are travelling together."

"No, I don't deny we are travelling by the same train. If you think that we are going together, you are at liberty to think so. You may draw your own conclusions. If you have no faith in me then that is the end of our friendship."

Tarun got confused. He realized with regret that he had committed a mistake in understanding Pramela.

"Pramela, I am sorry if I have offended you," he whispered.

"Well, I have nothing more to say to you Tarun and no apologies to offer," she said.

"But Pramela dear, you may at least explain the situation."

"I have nothing to explain. I have already written in quite a detail before I started this journey. You will receive my letter when you reach Delhi. Now if you think I am going to Jabalpur with Vicky, you free to have no interest in the future with me, the type of girl you would not like to associate yourself with."

"But look here Pramela, I realize I was wrong. But I am extremely worried about you all the same," said Tarun.

"Please try to understand and explain me all the circumstances."

The train was about to leave, she hurried and boarded the train and took her seat. Tarun followed her into the train.

"The train is about to leave. You should better go unless you want to travel with me," said Pramela.

"But Pramela, I would...."

"Good-bye Tarun, you have already done a lot for me and I am grateful to you. But please do not bother me any further. I think I can look after myself quite well. We will remain friends but nothing more."

"I will write to you," he murmured. "We must remain good friends. And by the way I came specifically to getting your signatures on certain papers."

With this he pulled out certain Documents from his briefcase. Pramela signed those papers hurriedly and again wished him good bye. He gave her a glance full of affection and rushed out of the train as the train was on the verge of leaving.

The journey was not quite comfortable for Pramela because of the heat and constant load of the passengers. But of late she had got accustomed to the rough life.

She got a lower berth in the compartment. Once it got dark, she tried to sleep. But the sleep eluded her. She kept thinking about what happened so suddenly this afternoon. She kept wondering. Why her life had become so undulated. Until the death of her father, she had no worry in life and there never was a moment for her to think about the rough life many people lead. But now was the period of her life wherein she had to think how bulk of the people lived under severe deprivation, many with no place to live, partial starvation, no opportunity for education etc.

On comparing she found that she was a million times happy; at least she was educated and sooner or later she would get a job. Life will take care of itself. She concluded that all she had to do was to train her mind to make the best use of opportunities God gave her and feel happy under any condition or situation. She did not know when sleep ultimately engulfed her.

She was still sleeping when the train reached Jabalpur. The movement and noise of the fellow passengers broke her sleep. Hurriedly she picked her luggage and got down. The restful sleep of the night, although relatively short, had comforted her exhausted body. She had only a light suitcase. She was on the verge of calling a porter to carry her suitcase outside the railway station to the taxi or auto rickshaw stand. But then she changed her mind; why not carry her luggage herself she thought. She had to go upstairs, tread the foot bridge and get down on the other side. This was the first occasion when she ventured to carry her luggage. She felt quite tired and exhausted by the time she reached the taxi stand. She had to halt for a couple of moments at two places in the process to catch her breath and to rest her body. She fully realized that it was mainly because she was not accustomed to it. But it was a good experience; she felt more confident about herself.

She was very eager to see her former governess. She instantly wanted to hire a cab. But that would have been costly for her. Cycle rickshaw, though cheap, would take a long time. She, therefore, hired an auto rickshaw, and gave the address to the driver.

She was completely unaware of the tragedy that had occurred in Tara's house. Actually she was living with her married elder sister, Mrs. Verma and husband, Vijaya Verma. It was a small house on the outskirts of the city, in residential complex on the road leading to the holy river Narmada. People were moving in and out of the house and there was a gloomy atmosphere there. She walked into a small sitting cum dining room. The furniture comprised of a few wooden chairs and a small centre table while the dining part included a small table with four chairs. The furniture was old but was made of teak wood and was well-polished. The room had an aura of economy combined with care and simplicity. Soon Tara came rushing and surprised her. There were tears in her eyes and she could hardly talk. She asked Pramela to be seated and then enquired about her journey.

"I am alright, only a little tired," said Pramela. "But what happened here?"

Tara had controlled herself until Pramela asked her.

She said, crying "My brother-in-law died yesterday; all of sudden."

"You mean your sister's husband? How did it happen?" asked Pramela.

Tara explained to her the circumstances under which her brother in law had died. She told Premela that he was a heart patient; And that he and his wife Vijaya had gone for shopping. It was a hot day and he over strained himself. On reaching home he complained of pain in his heart and before he could be taken to the hospital, he collapsed.

Pramela was shocked to learn about this incident. But soon she composed herself and consoled Tara. After a while, Tara arranged tea for Pramela and then asked her to freshen up. A room was reserved for her.

However Pramela realized that under the present condition it would not be appropriate for her to stay with Tara; in spite of all persuasions. Already several relatives had reached there and were staying in Tara's home. More were to come for the final rites on the thirteenth day. But at the same time she could not leave the town until the final rites were over. She therefore thought it fit to shift to some nearby hotel and meanwhile decide what to do perhaps she may be able to get a suitable job and she may shift to Tara's place eventually. She told Tara about her plan but promised that she would visit her daily. With a heavy heart, Tara agreed for it but asked Pramela to stay for lunch and shift to hotel only in the afternoon. To this Pramela agreed.

Tara suggested a moderate class hostel by the name Vasant Lodge in the vicinity of her home. It would be a small moderately furnished room with attached toilet. And that was all that Pramela needed. Moreover she had to spend economically as her funds were continually getting depleted.

Tara had to tend to work and as such she had very little time to talk to Pramela. However she got a general picture of all that happened after the death of Seth Dina Nath. Tara was deeply attached to the family and to Pramela in particular, she sincerely hoped that Pramela would agree to live with her after the rites were over.

Pramela chatted with the rest of the family members, relatives and guests of Tara. To her discomfort, she found herself as the centre of attraction and respect despite the fact that fate had reduced her to being almost pauper. To some extent she did enjoy the special attention but she felt that sooner or later the general euphoria will die and she will become a commoner. In her heart she was looking forward to that day when she would be treated as equal, and then only, she thought, she might enjoy the company.

Soon after tea and some talk over the tea table, Pramela took bath and got fresh. The dining table at Tara's home could accommodate only four at a time. Hence people ate in groups. After lunch she retired to her room and lied down for a while. However, soon she entered into deep sleep caused by the exhaustion of the journey.

She woke up late in the afternoon. She felt guilty and jumped up with a start. Evening tea was ready and was being served at the dining table. The table had a good spread of snacks. Pramela washed her face and walked to the dining room. All the chairs were occupied Tara pulled out another chair for her. She sat down and casually looked around. She knew everybody except one elderly couple seated next to her. Instinctively she bowed to them and introduced herself. The couple nodded, the elderly gentleman Dr. Kansal put his hand on her head to bless her. She realized that her introduction was not really needed, as she had already been talked about.

"I am Dr. Kansal, a retired Professor and she is my wife, also a retired professor," said the elderly man. "We both were working in Delhi and have moved here and running a coaching institution just to keep ourselves occupied."

"I am also from Delhi," murmured Pramela.

"Although we never met you before, my daughter Rashmi knows you. She was in your college, but senior to you. She got married last month to an engineer in central services and is currently posted at Allahabad."

"I am so glad to meet you both. I remember that I have met Rashmi on several occasions," said Pramela.

"I am so sorry to know about the sad and sudden demise

of your father. I understand that you want to take up a job," said Dr. Kansal.

"That is true uncle. *Amma*, sorry, I mean Mrs. Tara, invited me here and it's certain that I will get a job here," said Pramela.

Pramela called Tara as *amma* (mother) as she was her caretaker and was like a mother to her. It was the tradition at the house of Seth Dina Nath to address every family help with reverence. Pramela was affectionate to Tara and hence this visit.

Kansals instantly liked Pramela.

"Are you looking for any specific type of job?" enquired Dr. Kansal.

"In fact, there was no question of taking up a job had my father been alive. I shall be happy with any job where I can perform with my B.Sc. qualification and a place of work where I can work with some respect," said Pramela.

"In that case, you may work with us. We are running a coaching institution. You can work as a receptionist or as the cashier. No special training is required."

Pramela was delighted at the prospect of working with the Kansal couple. She readily accepted the offer.

"When can I join the duty then?" enquired Pramela.

"Any time, say tomorrow morning," said Dr. Kansal.

"I will do that. Meanwhile I will shift to a hotel this evening and make myself comfortable."

"We can help you with that as well. We have a sizeable big residence with two self-contained guest rooms. You can occupy one if you are comfortable."

"That would be marvellous," said Pramela. "But I would not like to be too much of a burden on you."

"You would not be a burden. On the contrary you would be an asset to us and also a company to Mrs. Kansal in your spare time."

"I don't know how to thank you uncle?" said Pramela with excitement and pleasure on her face. "I can hardly believe this is true."

"You don't have to thank us. The arrangement is for our mutual benefit. You will, no doubt, get a job of your liking, your independent room to live in and protection," said Dr. Kansal. "But we in return get an educated, cultured, and efficient worker for the institution and an excellent companion for Mrs. Kansal."

All this while, Tara had been a silent listener. She approved the arrangement. She knew the Kansal couple quite well and was certain that Pramela will enjoy both the work and the stay with the couple Of course several things remained silent such as the salary, arrangement of food for Pramela etc. But she preferred to leave it to them. She knew that salary had no special significance for Pramela. All she wanted was just enough to live and be reasonably comfortable.

Pramela also felt that in the future she could live on her own with no great obligation and let the future take care of her.

The silence was broken by Pramela.

"*Amma*, do I have your permission to accept the offer of Dr. Kansal?" asked Pramela.

"I am delighted," said Tara. "It is a great burden off my chest. Finding a suitable job and a suitable place of living for a young lady is quite a job by itself."

Soon she took Tara's leave and left with the Kansal couple. Their residence was only at a short distance from Tara's place. The house was built at the centre of a large piece of land. In the front, there was a beautiful lawn filled with flowers. The back yard had a kitchen garden and servant quarters. While designing the layout, they had taken care to provide accommodation for servants. Three separate medium sized rooms with a common toilet. Domestic servants become difficult to get and usually they come and go. An accommodation was a great incentive for them. Further the Kansal's paid them well and treated them well. As a result they were quite comfortable and satisfied. They had three full time helpers including a car driver, cook and general help. Both of them had retired from government service at Delhi and were drawing pension that was enough for their comfortable living. But to keep themselves busy, they had started this small institution at a short distance from their residence. They employed other teachers and an attendant and a clerk-cum-typist to assist them.

On reaching the residence, Pramela was shown her room. It was much better than what she had expected, an air conditioned well furnished room with marble floor and smooth walls with pleasing emulsion paint. Kitchen was also well designed and so was the bathroom.

Pramela changed into fresh clothes. Somebody knocked on the door and with her permission entered Ramu, a middle aged man of about 45 years of age who had been serving the Kansal couple since they had shifted to Jabalpur. He had a tray in hand with tea and biscuits. He placed the same on the table.

She switched on the fan and relaxed on the soft bed. There were few magazines lying on the central table. She picked up one and scanned through it in order to pass some time. Pramela sipped the tea and continued reading. Soon it was evening and she contemplated on going out for dinner to nearby restaurant. But she realized that she was not hungry. She had eaten a lot in the afternoon and just had tea and biscuits here. She, therefore, preferred to skip dinner. But her chain of thought was broken by a knock on the door. Again Ramu entered the room and informed her that *sahab* (Sahib) and *mem sahab* (Madam Sahib) were expecting her for dinner. This was yet another surprise and she was not expecting this extended courtesy. After all she was nothing but their employee.

She thought of changing her clothes but decided to go with what she was wearing, *salwar-kameez*. Dr. Kansal was seated on the chair at the head of the dining table that had six chairs. Mrs. Kansal was seated on an adjacent chair next to her husband. Pramela on entering the dining room nodded to pay her respect.

"Welcome my child, please take your seat," said Dr. Kansal, indicating the chair adjacent to him on the side opposite to Mrs. Kansal. There was an atmosphere of peace and quiet in the room. Dishes were put on the table and crockery for three had been laid on as well.

Pramela was searching for proper words to thank them. "I was just contemplating to go to the restaurant for dinner. It has been a pleasure being invited to dine here with you both. I sincerely feel thankful, but I will prefer not to bother you," said Pramela.

"Oh, forget about it. It is no botheration. You are not just an employee but also a guest. Hence you will live here as a member of the family and participate in all activities of the household including meals," said Dr. Kansal. Pramela was lost for words to either thank or protest. However she murmured, "If it is an order, I hardly have any choice, but you will have to excuse my inadequacy."

"It will be our pleasure. Now please help yourself and forget about all other matters."

Dinner was soon over, and they all shifted to the lounge. It was customary to have a cup of coffee after dinner time and then retire to bed.

She learnt during the course of conversation about the other servants besides the one she knew. Thus Ramu's wife Kamla worked as cook and cleaned the utensils. They lived in one room of the servant quarters. They had no children. The other room was occupied by Mali, Govind and his wife Asha who swept and mopped the house, dusted the furniture, and also washed the clothes. They had a kid Sukhlal about seven years of age who attended school. The third room was occupied by driver Kishan. Meals for Ramu and his wife were cooked in the kitchen. They took their meals in the bungalow itself. They were highly devoted to the family and in a way formed an extended family. Expenses incurred on all these accounts were quite high but Kansals could afford it. Besides their pension, they earned well from the institution.

Pramela realized that under these conditions, addition of one more member to the family was not a great burden to the old couple. Of course, Pramela was happy, and she looked forward to enjoy her stay there.

Before going to sleep, Pramela wrote a letter to Tarun, about the death of Tara's brother-in-law, about her meeting the Kansal couple and about her stay with them.

The students of the institution were either working people or students from various colleges. First batch of students attended classes from 9 am. The working hours were from 9 am to 1 pm and from 5 pm to 7 pm. It was not a heavy work schedule. Dr. Kansal had deliberately kept it light since he did not want to strain himself or his wife too much.

On the first morning after shifting to the new residence, Pramila woke up on hearing a knock on the door. It was around 6 am. Ramu had come to enquire if she would take the morning tea in her room or in the lawn with Sahib and Madam Sahib. She preferred to go to the lawn to join the couple. She took about ten minutes to get ready and walked to the lawn and wished the couple good morning.

"Good morning, my child," replied Mr. Kansal. "Please sit down and enjoy your tea."

Pramela took one of the vacant garden chairs facing the couple and prepared tea for all three of them. "How much sugar would you take uncle?" enquired Pramela.

"We both take only half a tea-spoon each," replied Dr. Kansal.

"So you have already taken over my role" said Mrs. Kansal. "Usually, I prepare the tea."

"It is my pleasure," said Pramela.

"We do not have diabetes but blood sugar is slightly on the higher side. Hence as a caution we have reduced the intake of sugar."

"My father used to take black tea with lemon during breakfast. Only in the office or on other occasions he would take tea with milk and little sugar," said Pramela. "I have picked up the same habit and enjoy black tea provided that the decoration is light."

"It is good to avoid sugar at our age. A little caution is always helpful," said Dr. Kansal.

Pramela first poured her cup of tea without stirring the decoction. It was light and very inviting. Subsequently she stirred the decoction and poured out two cups, added milk and sugar as directed and offered it to the old couple. She took liberty to ask Ramu to get half a lemon which she squeezed in her cup of tea. She did not add either sugar or salt.

The slight cool breeze flowing across the lawn was very pleasant. Pramela took few sips of the delicious tea with great satisfaction and took a biscuit along with her tea. The Kansal couple did not take any biscuit or nuts placed on the table. Mrs. Kansal observed that Pramela had taken a biscuit only and no other items.

"Pramela, do you want anything else with tea?" "No, thanks," replied Pamela. "I usually have a biscuit or two with the morning tea. It is unusual but *amma* (Tara) always insisted that I should not take tea on empty stomach. I do not know if there is any harm. But now it has become a habit."

"There is always some truth in these old sayings," said Dr. Kansal, "Usually, these customs are formed after a long observation. Thus a strongly brewed tea contains not only caffeine but other chemicals such as nicotine etc. which tend to irritate the stomach. Perhaps that may be the reason why one prefers eating something before or along with tea."

All the same they enjoyed their tea and had a light conversation.

"It seems like ages since I had my morning cup of black tea in such a pleasant surrounding," remarked Pramela. But she also felt a bit depressed at the thought of her father in whose company she used to have her morning tea and breakfast.

Mrs. Kansal looked at Pramela's face and realized how much must she would have suffered since the death of her father.

Once the tea was finished, Ramu removed the crockery. A little later they dispersed to get ready for breakfast scheduled at half past eight. Tight schedule was maintained as classes must start punctually.

Pramela was ready by 8 am and waited for others to arrive at the dining table. Her room was so located that she got a good view of the dining room. Breakfast was laid on the table by 8.30 am and Pramela, having overcome her hesitation, walked into the dining room. She took only a light breakfast. The driver was ready with the car and together they reached the Institute a little before nine.

Pramela felt a little nervous about the job. She initially was to work as a receptionist. The details of her job were explained to her by her lady colleague. She needed to receive the telephone calls, answer the enquiries, or to divert the same to the chamber of the Kansal couple. She would attend to the enquiries of various visitors regarding working hours, fee and scope of coaching, and also advise on which course to attend. She would also be required to advise about the nature of jobs available after the training and the various placement opportunities. In case of any difficulty she would refer them to her senior colleague or the Kansals.

For lunch she returned home along with the Kansals, ate lunch with them, and enjoyed the post lunch rest. Similarly she accompanied the Kansal couple for the evening session.

The dinner was served at about 8 pm. This became a normal routine and soon Pramila became like a member of the family. She was like a daughter to the couple.

Pramela called on Tara regularly as the family was mourning and she wanted to be a support at this time. She, along with the Kansals attended the thirteenth day ritual. Once the relatives left for their homes, Tara was left with only her sister. She again offered Pramela to come and stay with her but the Kansal couple insisted on the stay of Pramela with them.

"I am thankful to you Tara for giving Pramela to us. She has almost filled the vacuum created by our daughter's marriage," said Mrs. Kansal.

Time passed on smoothly for Pramela. Once she had settled down, she wrote a letter to Tarun relating all the events and her present occupation. She also apologized for her rough behaviour on the eve of her departure from Lucknow.

At the end of the month, Kansals offered her the salary.

"I get everything here in addition to your love. What more can I want?" said Pramela.

"You live here as our daughter. Hence whatever facility you get is your natural right. The salary is as compensation for the work you do."

"You treat me as your daughter. Then the question of salary does not arise. You would not pay your daughter had she worked in the institution," said Pramela.

"Perhaps not, But you do need money for your personal expenses."

"I will ask for money when I need. Can you please keep it with you," said Pramela.

The matter ended there. Pramela enjoyed both her stay at the residence of Dr. Kansal and the work. When she would get free she would often join in conversation with the old couple.

One evening the conservation turned to the life style of servants. "Our country is a big conglomeration of people of different religions, social customs, living habits and life patterns," said Mrs. Kansal. "The main stream of culture and social values is maintained from the Vedic period to this date by people of middle class. Life style is very different for persons of economically backward classes particularly the tribal people."

Mrs. Kansal paused for a while.

"Please continue, I feel interested," said Pramela.

"For instance we belong to upper middle class, educated and respected in society. As per tradition, our marriage was arranged by our parents. The most important factor was the family background. Ideally the families should be educated, well cultured and of similar financial standards. For the bride groom the desirable qualities include education, good behaviour, nature, employment and income. For the bride, the desirable factors are education, culture, proficiency in house hold work and adaptive nature. Of late greater emphasis is given to the looks; the boy should be tall and handsome while the girl should be tall, fair, and beautiful. In several cases, another important factor is the dowry presented by the parents of the girl to the parents of the boy. In our marriage we have high compatibility concerning education, culture, behaviour etc. No dowry was demanded. But jewellery, clothes and few other items were presented as it was customary. I took up a teaching job soon after marriage. Our marriage can be considered to be a typical traditional marriage and we have a good understanding. There are always some differences of opinions and some misunderstandings but these are usually sorted out. Divorce in our society is a sin even today."

"What could be the reason for this?" interrupted Pramela. She was enjoying the conversation and wanted to know more.

"There are several reasons: First, the girls are pushed by her parents particularly the mothers to live with harmony in the family of the bridegroom, to pay respect to the elders and to be helpful and faithful to the husband. Secondly, our divorce law (for Hindus) are rigid and also permits enough time for rethinking. It may take years together if divorce is contested by the other party. Finally, it is difficult for the divorcee to remarry; a social stigma gets attached to the persons. By and large, husband and wife, need to be able to adjust to the needs of the other and live in harmony. In many cases, children become the binding force and there is always a compromise."

"So you think arranged marriages have better chances of being more successful?" asked Pramela.

"I did not say so precisely. Love marriages, which are increasing in number each day, may be equal or more successful provided the marriage is for true love and not mere infatuation or show of love by one person for a rich spouse. Love is blind, they say, but so is disharmony and hatred. It is necessary to use the mind to fully fathom the compatibility of the match."

Pramela realized with regret how true the words of Mrs. Kansal were. Her love for Vicky formed a glaring example of a one way love. She had been duped. She had decided not to get fooled again. If at all she got emotionally attached to someone again, which she doubted, she would be very careful.

"What about people who are rich or very rich," asked Pramela.

"There are variations. The established rich families have their own traditions. Such families are essentially conservative but permit reasonable latitude to young people to mix in the society; even to make friends but have no physical intimacy. A line is drawn, but of course there are exceptions. Perhaps your family conforms to this category," said Mrs. Savita Kansal.

"I am inclined to agree with you. I have been allowed enough freedom and money but not physical intimacies. Great importance is attached to the purity of girls," said Pramela.

"That is good of you. Things are very different amongst very rich or even nouveau-rich class. The parents bring up their children blindly following the western culture. I do not intend to criticize them but the social condition that prevails is different in our country. Thus a young boy would go for dating with one or more girls and indulges in unacceptable behaviour too. But at the time of marriage, he wants one who is pure as honey and perfect for his family. The girls indulging in dating are, in general, the losers. This works in the west but not true for India – perhaps things might be different after 50 to 100 years. By then the social values in the west may perhaps change and tend to approach what we have in our country today. Social cycle is not static; it is changing and tends to revert to the older system."

"How about the very poor?" enquired Pramela curiously.

"Customs vary from place to place and from community to community. But in general, there is a greater freedom on both pre marital intimacies, and extra-marital affairs. Wife beating is a common practice. Why go far, our gardener Govind consumes country liquor every evening, rather a large dose and on coming home beats his wife without any provocation. It has become a sort of ritual. His wife Asha cries, uses abusive language on her husband, causing further pre-vocation and resulting in further beating. After some time, the entire episode ends, they eat together as if nothing happened."

"Why don't the neighbour Ramu or driver Krishan innerve?" asked Pramela innocently.

"Krishan tried once to stop the beating and accused Govind. But Asha shouted at him and asked him to mind his own business. It is entirely their family affair and no one can interfere. Once I probed Asha concerning the matter. She said that this has been a tradition in their community; no wife minds it. She went to the extent of saying that she rather enjoyed getting beaten by her husband."

"How very funny," remarked Pramela.

"Once Asha came and was filled with tears," said Dr. Kansal.

"I asked her what happened. She said, last night Govind came a little late, of course heavily drunk but did not thrash her. She was feeling perturbed and thought perhaps Govind no longer loved her and has started having an affair with some other woman. This continued for a couple of days and one night he did not come home at all but came in the morning with another woman much younger in age and good looking. Asha had no choice, she accepted her as the concubine of Govind."

"But isn't she living here now?" enquired Pramela. "No, she left after about a fortnight saying Govind was not a good match for her and she failed to get full satisfaction and that is how the episode ended."

It was getting late in the evening and Mrs. Kansal and Pramela proceeded towards the dining room.

Time passed on further; happily for Pramela. She had enough free time in the institute. She used this to learn typing with the help of her colleagues.

About three months later she received a letter from Tarun informing her that the assets of her father were fully mobilized, loans had been paid off and she was left with a small amount of money and also an agricultural land. He had written, "I will feel happy if you could come to Delhi for a few days, take charge of the assets and also discuss what to do with the land. My mother is also keen to meet you."

At first she thought of fixing this visit for a later date. She discussed the matter with Mrs. Kansal who advised her to go immediately and come back at her convenience.

"Don't worry about the work here," advised Mrs. Kansal. "A short break will be good for you." Mrs. Kansal handed her a packet of currency notes saying that the same might be useful to her in case of any emergency. With great reluctance Pramela accepted the packet. Having made up her mind, she proposed to start for Delhi the next day. But before going, she paid a visit to Tara and her sister.

Next day Pramela boarded the train for Delhi. Dr. Kansal had paid for and arranged a berth for her in an AC sleeper coach. The Kansal couple came to the railway station to see her off. On reaching her bogie, Pramela placed her suit case and air bag below her berth. She had kept enough drinking water in a thermos and packed food for dinner in the evening. Though food was usually available in the trains but the quality was generally poor. After placing her luggage she came to the platform to join the Kansal couple. There was still fifteen minutes for the train to depart. A moment later, she saw a tall, well built, handsome young man approaching them, a porter was carrying his luggage. He greeted the couple good afternoon and bent to touch their feet to pay his respect.

"Nice meeting you, Suri," said Dr. Kansal. "How are you?"

"I am fine sir, I came to attend my cousin's wedding. My niece and my father are going back to Delhi."

Dr. Kansal introduced him to Pramela.

"He is Surjeet Khanna, one of my students. He is in the Army," said Dr. Kansal. "She is Pramela, also from Delhi and now staying at Jabalpur. She is also going to Delhi for a brief visit."

"I will put my luggage in the compartment and be back in a minute," said Suri.

Meanwhile Dr. Kansal ordered for some cold drinks. Suri was back by the time the cold drinks arrived.

"What is berth number?" enquired Suri.

"It is twenty-three," said Pramela.

"What a stroke good luck. You are seated next to me," said

Suri in a hilarious mood. "My berth is twenty two."

Pramela found him well-bred, attractive and instantly developed a liking for him. While taking her cold drink, Pramela watched him through her beautiful lashes and judged him to be in his late twenties But he had a smile of a boy, spontaneous and enchanting.

"Take care of her," said Dr. Kansal to Suri.

"My pleasure," said Suri. The two boarded the train which soon started crawling.

Pramela and Suri were seated on opposite berths. Silence prevailed for some time which was then broken by Suri.

"It is unusually hot this year at Jabalpur," said Suri.

"Indeed," said Pramela being a little conscious.

"How are you related to the Kansal family?" asked Suri.

"No relation at all, but they are almost like parents to me," said Pramela. She was not very communicative and wanted to restrict herself to just answering the question without volunteering any information. Not replying would have accounted to rudeness.

"So you came here on a short vacation," asked Suri with an intention to draw her into conversation and to enjoy the pleasure of hearing her and relishing an occasional glance at her face. Pramela was deliberately acting aloof to present herself from the all-pervading charm of this young handsome man. She had suffered miserably because of Vicky and she was not mentally prepared for any further involvement with anyone. It was, of course, a strenuous job for her not be drawn by his magnetic personality completely enveloping the atmosphere. Any other girl would have instantaneously jumped into an intimate response by this time.

Her heart was, however, gradually overpowering her mind.

"I came here in search of a job," she replied. "Then came across the Kansal couple who were very nice to me. They not only employed me in their institute but also persuaded me to live with them as their guest. I am so very grateful to them."

He could not fully comprehend with the situation. "What made you take up a job at this tender age," he asked. "You evidently belong to a rich and sophisticated family. How could your parents permit you to do this?"

On the mention of her parents by Suri, she suddenly lost her control and tears trickled from her eyes in spite of her effort not to lose her calm. He realized that she was passing through a period of extreme mental torture and the stay at the Kansal's had only temporarily unknotted her nerves. But before she could control herself to reply, Suri apologized for having inflicted such a pain on her.

"I am sorry to have disturbed you so much," said Suri.

"I only asked out of curiosity. But please compose yourself." But he could not help her and so added in a lighter vein, "You look even more charming under distress."

Pramela noted the words of praise which she richly deserved. She looked at the somewhat disturbed and childishly anxious face of this charming man and replied,

"I have no parents and no home today. I lost my mother when I was a small child and lost my father a few months back. And because of his debt I had to give up all our property and the mansion where we lived. There is only a small agricultural land left. I am going to Delhi on a brief visit to take a stock of the situation and to decide about our land." She had shared all the information in the spur of the moment. She, in her mind, surmised that like Vicky, this young was enchanting and would cease to take any further interest in her once she had told about her present pecuniary and social position.

But that was not so.

"I am so sorry to know of what happened. Please forgive me for probing into your merciless past," said Suri. "You must have put up with all that with fortitude."

"There is nothing to forgive. It was all destined. It is wise to forget the past and take care of the present."

"I feel proud and honoured to know you and to be your friend. You are simply being marvellous and you are riding a high tide," said Suri.

"Please don't pity me," she blurted. "I will be all right and will try and make my life as purposeful as possible."

But you are unaware of the vile ways of the world.

"Certainly not so young that I cannot take care of myself," she said with all the seriousness she could muster. "I will turn twenty one in a few months."

"You certainly can take care of yourself, I agree," said Suri.

"But you have not told me anything about you," said Pramela.

"I am Surjeet Khanna, Major Surjeet Khanna to be precise. I have just completed my term as a short service commissioned officer and have been offered permanent commission. I have yet to decide whether to accept it or not. Currently I am on a long leave and will decide by the end of the month."

"You already know my name. I am daughter of late Seth Dina Nath, then a business magnate."

"My father was also in the army; retired as a colonel at a rather young age. We purchased a plot of land in Green Park, and built a small house with whatever money he got on retirement. We were reasonably comfortable but not rich."

"Oh, how does that matter in life whether you are rich well-to-do or just middle class? What matters is just the peace of mind and your ability to enjoy life in whatever circumstance God has preferred to keep you," quipped Pramela.

"You have learnt a lot at this young age," he remarked.

"That is the virtue of adversity and poverty. I have seen the two extremes of life, the very rich and very poor. Believe me, after the death of my father and loss of property, I have enjoyed the adversity equally or perhaps more. You see people in their real and natural states when you are low, not with a coating of false show of affection," said Pramela.

"You have become a good judge of human behaviour. What is your opinion about me?" asked Suri.

"You are upright, honest and an adorable person," said Pramela frankly, but soon realized the significance of her remarks.

"Thank you very much. I feel like a boy who has cleared his test."

"Oh, don't be naughty," she said.

"But one thing is certain. I can bank on your friendship."

"Well, I will feel happy," she said.

"The train will reach Delhi early morning. Will you come for a drive with me in the evening?" he asked.

"Well I don't know if I can."

"Are you already engaged for the evening?"

"No, but I am not certain about anything. I don't know where I will be putting up."

"You mean you are absolutely on your own," he blurted out.

"Yes I am. I have no close relative, no friend whom I can rely on. Perhaps relations change overnight once they know your financial status."

"But you can't be on the road," he said with real concern in his eyes.

Pramela gave a subdued laugh and told him about Vijay Singh, Savvy and Tarun Gupta.

"How about your solicitor, Tarun, is he a good and a dependable friend?"

"He has been the family solicitor. He is reliable and dependable," replied Pramela evading the status of their friendship.

"You would dine with me tomorrow evening, won't you? We may discuss matters further," said Suri.

Pramela got disarmed by his persistent and genuine offer.

"I can do that if you are sure that you will be free," she said.

"I shall be free," said Suri.

For the rest of the evening in the train, they talked on topics of general interest, politics, sports, film etc. and enjoyed the scenery. Around 8 pm, they took dinner, wished each other good night and stepped on their respective berths.

The train reached Delhi at about 8 am the next morning. They got down and were to take separate taxis.

"Shall we meet at about 8 pm, say at Café Plaza?"

"I shall be there," said Pramela.

He hired a taxi for Pramela, and helped her with the suitcase in the taxi.

"Which destination shall I tell the driver," asked Suri.

"As I said I don't know," said Pramela laughingly.

Suri took it seriously and became worried about her safety and said, "If you do not know your destination, I suggest I must choose one for you. You are coming to my place."

"But I was only joking," said Pramela, "For the time being I am going to the working women's hostel, off Lodhi Road."

"But will you get an accommodation there?" asked Suri.

"No, I will stay with the superintendent as her guest but only for few days. This is a special privilege granted by her to me. I have stayed in the hostel after my father's death."

It was his turn to be surprised.

"You are certainly able to influence people," he said.

"Thanks for the compliment," said Pramela. She asked the driver to proceed and waved to Suri.

After she had driven off, he remained standing in deep thought for quite some time and realized with a start that for the first time in his life he was in love, and that too at the first sight.

Desperately in love with a girl whom he had known for such a short time, a girl with no home or position or money but highly enchanting and full of courage and self-respect. He had vowed not to marry any girl whom he did not love deeply and he had set his standards very high. As a result he had come across numerous girls too willing to love him, but none came up to his expectation. But this was a sudden and surprising experience. He failed to understand himself. He had decided to see her more and marry her if she would.

Pramela returned to the hostel. She loved to stay there but she knew she could perhaps stay there only for a brief time. And her visit too was designed to be brief. She would complete her work in Delhi and go back to Jabalpur where she worked with the Kansals. On reaching the hostel premises, she went straight to meet the superintendent Mrs. Prasad and told her about her plans. Mrs. Prasad was glad to receive her and made the necessary arrangement for her stay in one room in her own suite.

On her arrival at Delhi, she had planned to call Tarun, but all her plans changed. She was anxiously looking forward for her dinner with Suri that evening. She decided to postpone calling Tarun.

Tarun, on the other hand, was anxiously looking forward for her visit to Delhi. He was a little upset after the unpleasant meeting he had with Pramela at Lucknow. He wildly longed for her but his feelings were not reciprocated. His hopes got refreshed on hearing from Pramela. He was glad, that she was living comfortably at Jabalpur. But he wanted to be near her and talk to her.

That morning when he received a letter with his address written in Pramela's own handwriting, his heart missed a beat and his face radiated with joy. The change was so obvious that both his mother and his cousin Suman became aware of the same and exchanged glances.

Suman was no blood relation to Tarun. As she grew to adulthood, her feelings towards Tarun started changing. No longer had she considered him as her cousin and she didn't harbour sisterly feelings towards him. Although she did not express her love for Tarun; her every action was designed to please him and she looked forward for the day when her love and devotion would be reciprocated.

While opening the letter from Pramela, Tarun said looking towards his mother, "This letter is from Jabalpur from Pramela." His mother looked pleased.

"What is she doing there?" asked Suman a little coldly.

"She is working as a receptionist cum accountant at an institution run by an elderly couple, Dr. Kansal and Mrs. Kansal, both retired professors from a college in Delhi."

"And where is she staying?" asked his mother.

"She is staying with the Kansals almost as a family member," said Tarun.

"That's funny," uttered Suman.

"What is funny about it? She seems to be well settled for the time being," said Tarun a little tersely.

Suman did not like the remarks but kept quiet.

Now second letter was received in response to one from Tarun concerning the financial matters. He did not expect Pramela to come so promptly but as per this letter she was expected to be in Delhi this morning. Where has she gone, he wondered. He felt elevated by the thought of meeting her and was equally concerned about her whereabouts. "She should have called me by now if she has reached Delhi this morning," said Tarun, a little disturbed. He looked at his mother for some comment. She was equally worried.

"I hope and wish she is all right," said his mother. "It is not safe now a days for girls to travel long distances all alone."

"I do agree," said Tarun in a depressed mood.

"Let us wait till tomorrow. If we do not hear from her, you better call up the people with whom she is staying at Jabablpur," said the mother.

"Yes I will do that," said Tarun gloomily.

But he knew that he would be worried throughout the day. His concern for Pramela was so great that he could not concentrate on his work the whole day.

In the evening he had to attend a get together with a few close friends at Café Plaza. He was not in a pleasant mood but he maintained his schedule and drove to Café Plaza. Already a few friends had arrived and others were expected shortly. It was a small group that met periodically at different places and enjoyed the evening together in an effort to do away with the fatigue of the work involving long days. A few were teetotallers while others enjoyed drinking. Tarun preferred beer. The drinks were served and they proceeded with general conversation.

Tarun had hardly taken a few sips of beer when he, to his great surprise, saw Pramela entering the café escorted by a tall, handsome young man. The head waiter led them to a table reserved for them in one corner of the room. It became apparent to Tarun that the young man was a frequent and valued visitor to this café. Pramela however did not notice Tarun as she passed his table. Tarun observed her walk with her usual light, graceful carriage to the table assigned to them.

He could not fail to notice several eyes turned to stare at her with high admiration. Her companion also looked so handsome and smart, that the two together become the centre of attraction. Tarun could not resist himself further. He took a short leave of his friends and walked towards the table occupied by Pramela and her companion.

Both Pramela and Suri were punctual and had reached the café almost simultaneously. Pramela had agreed to the offer of Suri with some initial inhibitions but once she reached the café, she wanted to enjoy herself fully. Surjeet Khanna was a charming person and she could see the warmth and affectionate admiration in his eyes.

"It is so very nice to be back in Delhi. Our own Delhi, hot, polluted and yet so compelling, enhanced in its charm further by the presence of such an enchanting girl by my side. This makes it even better," said Suri.

Pramela acknowledged the greeting with a nod and simply said, "Yes, it is so wonderful to be back. But I am only on a short visit and I must go back to my work at Jabalpur. I am so very comfortable there and have such wonderful people to take care of me but Delhi has its own charm. Perhaps it is in the blood."

"I fully acknowledge of what you are saying. How is your stay at Jabalpur?" said Tarun having come upto their table.

Pramela turn to look at the new corner.

"Tarun," she exclaimed in a surprised and pleasant voice.

"It is a pleasant surprise seeing you here. When did you come? I have been expecting you since this morning," said Tarun.

Pramela was flooded with these entire questions. She thought she owed him an explanation. However she kept her calm and said in a pleasant voice.

"My stay at Jabalpur has been quite comfortable as I mentioned in my letter. As per schedule, I reached Delhi this morning and intended to see you tomorrow morning."

Suri thought, "So this is the family solicitor, a rather nice and jolly fellow."

"Me and my mother both were very worried since you did not contact us since morning. In fact I decided to call Dr. Kansal about you. I wondered, perhaps you had postponed your programme about coming from Jabalpur," said Tarun in a calm voice.

But Pramela preferred to evade the question.

"May I introduce you to Major Surjeet Khanna? Mr. Tarun Gupta, our family friend and solicitor."

Both shook hands and exchanged greetings.

"So this is Tarun, the solicitor Pramela had been talking about," thought Suri. They remained quiet for a few odd moments, assessing each other. Pramela, however, broke the silence.

"I came back this morning only and I will see you tomorrow morning in your office if that will suit you."

Tarun expected a little more informal reply. He preferred her to come to his residence. But, he was happy that at least tomorrow he will be able to talk to her for long. In the presence of this new friend Surjeet Khanna, talking to Pramela may not be possible.

"I will be available in the first half of the day. Do come as per your convenience," said Tarun and he left and joined his group after taking leave of Pramela and Major Khanna.

"A bright young man, your lawyer, Mr. Tarun," remarked Suri.

"Yes, he is smart, intelligence and expert in his work. He has been really devoted to our family."

Once Tarun had left for his table, Pramela and Suri switched the talk to their mutual concern.

Suri talked about his family, his service in the army and his future employment. All the time he was extremely charming to Pramela. She mostly listened to him giving him some information about her family life, about her father and his business.

The evening was good. Both enjoyed each other's company. It was quite late in the night, when they had their dinner.

Suri was full of enthusiasm and looked forward to meeting her again.

"I believe in luck. Our meeting at the railway platform at Jabalpur was also a stroke of good luck for me," he said with all sincerity. "What are we? Just toys in the hands of God. It is prudent to make the best use of the situation afforded to us by the Almighty."

"I do also believe in destiny. Major events in our life are destined. We, however, have to play our role to the fullest," said Pramela.

"You are so nice, charming and brave, keeping your self-respect in the most difficult situation. But I am quite worried about you. Don't you feel miserable at times?"

"It was so immediately after the death of my father and financial ruin for the family. But this time has toughened me and I now take life as it comes," said Pramela.

"I have no words to describe my admiration for your

brave behaviour," said Suri. "But with all the efforts put by you, I feel you are quite miserable."

"Oh no, I am happy under the circumstances, the Almighty has preferred to place me in."

Their evening together was coming to an end. An evening both enjoyed and wanted to continue. Suri proposed that they meet again next evening to which Pramela agreed readily.

"I will look forward to our evening tomorrow," said Suri.

"I have to see Tarun in the morning and look into my financial matters. Further he will arrange to sell my car which I do not need any longer," said Pramela with a heavy heart.

Suri could understand the pain suffered by her. Parting with her personal things, inanimate that had become part of her life. To part with such an item inflicted pain almost of some magnitude as if parting with one's near and dear.

They came out; Suri hired a taxi and dropped her to the hostel. Suri came out to bid her good night and to get a promise from her that she would call him to confirm the evening appointment for next day. As the taxi departed taking Suri to his residence, Pramela kept standing seeing him go and finally with an effort entered her room.

Next morning Pramela went to Tarun's office. As soon as she entered the room, blood rushed onto Tarun's face, he was madly in love with her but could not muster the courage to express it. He was in a state of extreme excitement and nervousness at the same time. He was also a bit disturbed at the thought of the other man the previous night, Major Suri. However, soon he regained his composure and welcomed her. He politely asked her to be seated. Pramela was, on the other hand, in her own way, teasing in spite of her precarious family and pecuniary condition.

"You look fresh and charming," said Tarun to start the conversation and to please her.

"At your service, my dear Tarun," said Pramela, "Please proceed and give me a general picture of where I stand."

"The same I had written to you about. Not much left except your personal belongings including your car and the agricultural land." He said, "You may retain the car or sell it."

"I prefer to sell it since I can't afford to maintain it. But I don't' know. I never thought about it in detail. What is your advice?" said Pramela.

"I propose, you retain it unless you need money badly."

"My needs are now very limited. I am already saving a pocketful," said Pramela and she described in considerable details her job and her residence with the Kansal couple at Jabalpur.

"I am glad and relieved to learn that you have good company and are free from financial worries to some extent." said Tarun, "In that case we may retain the land. Prices of land are moving up fast and you stand to gain in selling it later."

"Please, choose what you deem fit," she said a little carelessly.

"Also I will arrange to lease out this land and you should get a small amount yearly."

"I don't know how to thank you," she said, "You are so helpful and so reliable."

She looked in his eyes directly and found an extremely tender but uneasy look in his eyes. He looked rather pale and uncertain. However, she could see the reason for the same.

"Are you all right Tarun?" she asked anxiously,

"I am ok, thanks."

He looked directly in her eyes and said, "I am sorry for what happened on the railway platform that day. I owe you an apology."

"It is alright; let us not go again into the incident. It is best to forget it."

"But I can hardly pardon myself," said Tarun. In fact the very presence of that Vicky infuriated me beyond my control."

"I respect you, my dear Tarun, forget about the incident," said Pramela, giving an uncomfortable laugh.

"I will try to."

"I can appreciate your anxiety," said Pramela, "You were my Daddy's friend and now my friend. But please do permit me to lead my own life."

"Yes, I should understand these circumstances."

"Further even if I had been going away with Vicky, I don't see any reason for you to get upset or to interfere in my personal matters," she said rather carelessly but soon repented.

He turned his face to her directly and she was shocked to see glistening of his eyes and was sure that he must be making efforts to prevent the tears from pouring out. Suddenly it occurred to her that he not just cared for her but loved her too. She looked at him but had nothing to say, she now realized the amount of mental torture he must be experiencing.

With great effort Tarun controlled himself.

"I have no right to interfere," he said rather hoarsely, "Absolutely no right, you are now grown up and on your own and owe me nothing. I was a fool to have made an effort to save you from the evil desires of Vicky."

Having said this he kept quiet. He faintly realized that he had given himself away. He had given away his true and selfless love for her. Pramela also kept quiet, reflecting over this sudden outburst of his feelings. She had always liked him and respected him but had never harboured any feeling of love for him.

"Let us not get all worked up," said Pramela, quickly, "I do admit, my meeting Vicky at the railway stations looked quite suspicious but believe me, he was the last person in the world I wanted to meet. I have already thrown away my relationship with him. In fact, I was on my way to Jabalpur to see my old governess, Tara, perhaps you remember her."

"Yes, I do. She left quite long back."

"I had planned to stay with her and search for a suitable job."

"I am sorry, I jumped to a wrong conclusion and made a fool of myself," said Tarun.

"When I reached Jabalpur, I found that Tara's brother-in-law had died of a sudden heart failure and I could not possibly stay with her and her sister."

"It must have been a terrible shock to you."

"It was indeed. But I am getting used to shocks, big and small. Fortunately I met Dr. Kansal and Mrs. Kansal, who not only provided me a job in their office but also a place to stay in their own house as their guest."

"That was one stroke of good luck for you."

"Yes, on hearing from you, I preferred to take a short leave to come to Delhi to meet you and look into my financial matters. However on the railway platform, I met Major Surjeet – Suri for short."

"I see. A lucky chap I must say."

Tarun felt a tinge of jealously but controlled himself not to show it.

Pramela then told Tarun the details of her train journey with Suri, about her dinner meeting with Suri and her proposed meeting with him that evening.

Tarun realized then that Pramela was once more in love, now with Suri. "How lucky are certain people," he thought with a stroke of jealously. How much he wanted to be in the shoes of Suri. With effort, he resigned himself to quietly harbouring feelings of love for Pramela. It was a strenuous effort on his part but he had by now got used to it. In his heart, he wished her well in her present time with Suri.

Having finished her business with Tarun, Pramela got up and took leave to go to her hostel.

Once again, Tarun offered her to come and stay with him, his mother and his cousin but she very politely declined the offer. She preferred her privacy.

"I wish you all the best in life once again," said Tarun as a parting gesture. "I hope you will be seeing me from time to time."

"Thank you for all the good wishes," said Pramela.

"I will certainly meet you but I myself don't know how long I will be staying in Delhi before returning to Jabalpur".

"You are certainly a brave girl; You have all my admiration," said Tarun.

"Thanks again," said Pramela with a feeling of goodwill and affection. "You are always so nice to me; I shall always remain grateful."

Affection and gratefulness are alright in their respective places, pondered Tarun. What he really longed was for the love of this wonderful girl and which evaded him all the time.

Pramela offered Tarun her hand as a gesture of goodwill.

This was unusual on her part. Tarun shook her hand with all the warmth he could muster.

Once Pramela left his office, he remained deeply in thought, pondering over his feelings towards her.

# CHAPTER 4

Pramela had her dinner appointment with Suri on the second day. The evening was very enchanting. They talked over different matters and phases of their lives and enjoyed listening to each other. They finished their dinner little early as they preferred to walk to the park nearby. In the silent atmosphere they continued their conversation interspersed with brief intervals of silence. They both felt that their meeting was destined by God for their union.

Time passed by, offering amazing opportunity to Pramela and Suri to meet constantly. They would usually meet at a specific time in the evenings at predetermined locations and spend their time together. But Pramela could not continue like this for long. She had to decide, if she wanted to go back to Jabalpur or seek a job in Delhi itself. She was getting short of funds, so she couldn't avail the facilities at the hostel much longer. Although Tarun had offered her to live with his family, but pride on her part did not permit her to accept the offer. She had to shift her residence.

Pramela applied at several employment agencies by submitting her resume. She had no previous work experience except the short stint at Jabalpur as receptionist-cum-cashier. One morning she received a call from Sunrise Employment Agency located at South Extension for an interview. To be on time, she woke up early in the morning and reached the office of the employment agency just as it opened. A well-built lady in her mid-forties, Mrs. Thakur interviewed her regarding her education, training, aptitude and experience.

"I find that you have no training and almost have no experience except a brief one as a receptionist," said Mrs.

Thakur. She looked somewhat puzzled as Pramela was very attractive and was well dressed.

Pramela preferred to remain quiet.

"There are two openings," said Mrs. Thakur. "One a travelling saleswoman and the other as a nursery school teacher. What would be your choice?"

"Kindly elaborate about the requirements of these jobs," said Pramela.

"As a travelling saleswoman, you would have to go door to door and sell vacuum cleaners. You will be given training on the operation of the equipment. You will also be acquainted with the merits of the equipment and a few tips about sales techniques. Also, you would be accompanied by an experienced saleswoman for few days and then you can operate independently. There will be a small fixed salary plus bonus on sales. Also it depends on how well you perform your work."

"How about the other job?" asked Pramela.

"As a nursery school teacher, you will be required to handle and teach a batch of nursery school children. The job is a little less tiring compared to that of a travelling saleswoman but the salary is fixed and relatively lesser," said Mrs. Thakur.

Pramela compared the two jobs and decided to accept the job as a teacher.

"I will prefer to work as a teacher," said Pramela, "What do I have to do? I have no previous experience or training as a nursery teacher."

"I know you would prefer to work as a teacher and I felt that teaching will suit you better. From your looks I understand that you are from a good family. You have good control over English language and have good manners. These are the prerequisites for this job. However to start with you will have to assist an experienced teacher and learn all that is needed.

Subsequently you can handle the students independently," said Mrs. Thakur.

Pramela mentally pictured herself in the nursery class with well dressed little kids. She thought she would enjoy this work better.

Her train of thoughts were broken by the stern voice of Mrs. Thakur.

"Well then, would you please report to Miss Ranjan, Principal, A.P. Kay Model School, Sardarjang Enclave?" "Yes," replied Pramela. "I think I will enjoy my work."

"I am sure you will," said Mrs. Thakur. "Here is the address."

Pramela came out of the employment agency's office. It was quite hot in the afternoon. She wanted to hire a taxi or an auto rickshaw like before, but she controlled herself as she wanted to accustom herself to save money and decided to travel by bus.

Slowly she walked to the bus-stand and waited for about five minutes before she could board the desired bus.

As she entered the bus, she found that the bus was already overcrowded. There were no empty seats available and about twenty people were already standing. She made a quick survey of the scene in the bus. Like all other standing passengers, she caught hold of the leather loop hanging from the bars.

At the next stop, the bus screeched to a halt abruptly and as a result a train of standing passengers lurched forward, in a way integrating the congregation of standing passenger into a monolithic mass swaying to the sudden change of speed.

Pramela felt awkward and suffocated but she gathered all her energy to face the inconvenience. "If all others can do it, why can't I?" was the thought paramount in her mind.

She was reminded of the words of a learned poet:

*"The waves of nursery and pain,*
*Let not dampen my spirit in vain,*
*Behold how thunders sheets of rain,*
*Soak the earth for better gain"*

The man standing next to her in the bus asked her about her destination. When she told him, he said, "You have taken the wrong bus. Please get down at the next stop, bus No. 302 will take you to the bus stop adjacent to the school building." She was grateful for his correct advise.

She did accordingly and finally reach the school. She was pretty exhausted from dust, heat and jerks from the rattling bus. She entered the school premises and asked for the principal, Miss Ranjan.

On entering the Principal's office, she found a rather good looking middle aged lady sitting in an enormous chair and scribbling on a sheet of paper. As Pramela entered, she smiled and asked Pramela to be seated.

"I have been expecting you for the last half an hour or so, Miss Pramela," said the lady, "Don't be surprised, the Sunrise employment agency had telephoned me about an hour back about you."

"I am here, slightly delayed, as I took the wrong bus and had to change bus on the way here," said Pramela.

"You are extremely young and fresh, and more enchanting that I had expected."

Pramela was a bit surprised at the out of place compliment but she ventured to say,

"I have come here for the job as a nursery school teacher."

"You stand employed and may join from tomorrow. The school working hours are from 8 am to 1 pm, but all the teachers are required to be here ten minutes early," said Miss Ranjan.

"It suits me," said Pramela.

"You have not asked about the salary. But I must tell you. To begin with your salary would be Rs. 3000 per month. However, once you start engaging classes independently, your salary will be increased depending on your performance."

"I will try to give my best," said Pramela.

"Here is your letter of appointment. I kept it ready assuming that you will agree to the proposal. Can you please fill this form by writing your home address and telephone number?"

Pramela filled the form and added her hostel address.

"So you already have a room in working women's hostel?"

"It is only on temporary basis for a week, in the mean time I have to search a suitable but humble accommodation for me," said Pramela for her information.

"If you are alone you can stay with me. I have my apartment in the college premises. I can spare you a room," said Miss Ranjan.

It was an un-expected gesture of benevolence. But Pramela had gone accustomed to unexpected things. She was however, hesitant in accepting the offer. Ranjan could see the hesitation prominently written on the face of Pramela. She further elaborated.

"I may have self-interest in the proposition, I am all alone and I am sure, you will prove to be a good company."

"I will be only too glad to accept your kind offer. But I want my own privacy," said Pramela rather apologetically.

"You will have your full liberty and privacy. The guest room which I propose to give you has access to the public road," persuaded Miss Ranjan.

The offer was too tempting to refuse. Further Pramela thought that she could change her residence anytime if the living conditions were not good.

That evening when she met Suri for dinner, she narrated all the events that happened during the day. Suri concurred with her decision. However, he insisted that she keep her evenings free for him instead of spending time with Miss Ranjan.

"You seem to be jealous of Miss Ranjan," teased Pramela.

"You are right. I hate to let anyone deprive of my evenings with you," said Suri rather excitedly.

Next morning Pramela joined her duty in the school. She shifted to the residence of Miss Ranjan in the evening.

That evening she did not go out with Suri as she got delayed shifting to her new residence and also had to arrange her room.

Next morning she slept longer as she was tired because of shifting. She woke because of a gentle knock at her door. A young maid brought a cup of tea.

"Breakfast will be ready at seven," said the maid Reena. "Anything specific thing you generally eat for breakfast?"

"No, nothing specific, I will join for breakfast on time," said Pramela.

She had not talked about her breakfast, lunch or dinner with Miss Ranjan, perhaps it was assumed. She got ready hurriedly and joined Miss Ranjan for breakfast. After breakfast, they walked about the school and to their respective class rooms. After school, Pramela returned to her room and was summoned for lunch. It was a simple lunch and Pramela enjoyed it. During lunch Pramela informed Ranjan that she usually went out for dinner with her friend Surjeet and could get late. Ranjan did not object to it. On the contrary she expressed her pleasure.

"At least you spend your evenings with good company," said Ranjan.

"Look at me; I have to pass the evening mostly with myself."

That evening Pramela left her room at the usual hour. She locked the door that opened to the road so that Ranjan was not disturbed. She planned to return early so that there was no room for objection from Miss Ranjan. But in the company of Suri, time flew faster than usual and again it was almost midnight before Pramela entered her room. Quickly she changed her clothes and prepared herself to retire for the night. She switched off the light and prepared herself to sleep.

Hardly five minutes had passed by, when Pramela heard a whisper in the adjoining room, the bedroom of Miss Ranjan with the lights off. At first impulse she thought of enquiring but on a second thought she preferred to keep quiet and understand what the matter was. After quite some time she observed the door of Miss Ranjan's bedroom open and a young well-built man in his early twenties come out and leave for the next apartment. Pramela had an uneasy sleep that night.

Next day after lunch as Pramela retired to her room to rest, Miss Ranjan accompanied her and sat on a chair. Obviously she wanted to talk to her.

"You came rather late last night," said Ranjan casually.

"Yes, our dinner got delayed."

"Did you have a sound sleep?"

"No, my sleep was disturbed by the conversation going on in your bedroom," said Pramela innocently.

"Yes, he is Romesh, accounts clerk in our school. He resides in the adjoining apartment" said Ranjan. "Are you shocked?"

"It is all new and disturbing."

"Naturally, you are young, and innocent. I have seen the vagaries of life and I am not averse to a few moments of pleasure that come my way," said Ranjan.

"But he is just a boy, almost like your son, had you been married. Don't you feel uncomfortable?"

"On the contrary, I enjoy every moment when I am with him. He is so young, simple and unmarried. When he feels lonely, he comes to me. More often I invite him."

"But is it only his company? Do you not go beyond that?" said Pramela hesitatingly, "I mean, do you not indulge in …?" and her voice trailed off.

"You are too simple, Pramela," said Ranjan teasingly.

"Do you think, I and Romesh confine ourselves only to

talking. We do go beyond that and I must say it is extremely enjoyable. I do not see anything immoral in it. I take it as a satisfying experience."

"But our social system condemns such amorous relations."

"That is the trouble with our social system. It is too rigid and ignores the basic needs of people. It needs radical changes. In the west, social systems are much more need based," said Ranjan.

"But why did you not marry?" asked Pramela.

"That is a long story," said Ranjan. "I belonged to a middle class family, three sisters and two brothers. The eldest sister got married during the life time of my father. He died leaving behind me, my sister, my mother, and two younger brothers. I had just then passed my MA examination. I wanted to go for research for my doctorate. But I had to give that up and take a job. I managed to educate and get my brothers married. By the time I was free from my family responsibilities, I was past thirty and well past the proper age of marriage. Since then I have reconciled to my fate."

"I can appreciate your plight," said Pramela, "But I feel even at the age of thirty you could have got a match, may be a widower or divorcee with average means. I mean it is better than not marrying at all."

"I differ on this count," said Ranjan. "I would rather not marry than to marry a person who is not to my liking. In fact, I had an association with one when I was around thirty two. But he cheated on me. He was after my money. Having collected whatever he could, on one pretext or the other, he vanished from my life leaving me with all the bitterness."

Pramela could only empathise with Ranjan. She could hardly appreciate the life she was leading. She however preferred to leave it to her so long as it did not influence her own life.

But it was not destined so. One Sunday, when Pramela joined Ranjan for lunch, she found Romesh also at the table. She disliked the situation but controlled herself from any direct conflict. After lunch Ranjan retired to her room but Romesh stayed on. When Pramela stood up to go to her own room, Romesh interrupted her.

"I want to talk to you on a matter of great significance," he said.

"Pray, proceed. I want to go and take a short nap."

"I will not keep you long," he said.

Pramela did not like him and his present conduct but to avoid any conflict she permitted him. Without any hesitation and preliminaries, he said, "I love you and want to marry you."

Pramela was taken aback.

"We have just met, we hardly know each other," she murmured.

"But I saw you at the lunch time and I was deeply impressed. I am sure, you will not disappoint me."

"Even assuming that you love me, I don't love you," said Pramela. "Hence the question of marriage does not even arise."

"You will start liking me as you come to know me better," he said.

Pramela, nonplussed by his rubbish talk, preferred to evade him.

"I will see to it when I need to," she said. To avoid further talks, she wished him good bye, entered her room and drew the curtains.

All this while, she had been meeting Suri in the evenings. She had call Tarun about her present occupation and residence.

But Tarun had been avoiding Pramela. She would have gone back to Jabalpur and enjoyed the excellent company of the Kansals, but was staying put because of the presence of Suri at Delhi. She was now so deeply attached to Suri that their marriage was quite eminent in the near future.

Her stay with Miss Ranjan got terminated due to a nasty incident one late evening. Miss Ranjan had planned to visit one of her brother's and stay there overnight. She told Pramela to keep the door adjoining the dining room bolted. Also she arranged for a night *chowkidar* at the apartment. Pramela as usual had her dinner with Suri and returned to her room slightly before midnight. She was on the verge of putting her sleeping gown when she heard knuckle knocks on the door joining the dining room. She thought that perhaps the *chowkidar* (watchman) wanted to say something. As soon as she opened the door, she saw Romesh rushing in. Pramela understood his intentions and mustered all her courage and presence of mind to tackle the situation.

"Will you please leave my room," she said rather authoritatively.

"I have come to talk to you."

"This is no time for talking. Besides I have already told you about my mind," said Pramela.

"Then I have no choice but to forcibly possess you."

She saw the demon in his eyes, but managed to keep her head cool.

"You can't do that, you know it fully well. I will shout and the *chowkidar* will be here in no time and also the neighbours."

"I have relieved the *chowkidar*. You certainly cannot shout. Your good name will be tarnished."

Pramela pondered over the situation and prepared herself for defence. Fortunately, while in school, she took courses in Judo and Karate for self-defence. She had not practiced it for quite some time but she could use her training now. She searched for a suitable time. As he reached within striking range, she acted with lightning speed bringing him to ground with a thud. It took him quite some time to assess the situation and he managed to rise with great effort.

"Now leave the room immediately," said Pramela with renewed self-confidence.

Without a word, he crawled out of the room. Pramela bolted the door and contemplated on the future course of action. As a first step, she decided to leave this room immediately. Miss Ranjan came in the morning and Pramela related to her the entire incidence and sought her permission to shift to a nearby hotel or apartment at the earliest. Miss Ranjan tried to dissuade her. She assured her that she would take enough care ensuring non-occurrence of such incidents in future. But Pramela remained firm on her decision. Accordingly Ranjan arranged for a one room apartment in a nearby lodge. Pramela shifted there in the afternoon. The room was furnished with a single bed, a wardrobe, writing table and two chairs. There was an attached toilet and a small kitchen. This was all she needed. It was further arranged that packed lunch would be sent to her room from the hostel kitchen of the school on usual payment. Pramela felt quite satisfied with the arrangement.

Pramela phoned Tarun to inform about her new arrangement. She also wrote to Kansals at Jabalpur informing about her new residence, the job and also about Suri in detail. She also wrote letters to Tara at Jabalpur, to her bua at Lucknow and her friend Savvy.

That evening Pramela related the incidence in full details to Suri. He got angry and felt like giving Romesh a good thrashing. However, Pramela pacified him.

"I have done the job on your behalf," she said. "He will never dare to make similar attempts towards any other woman in future."

"You are a brave girl. I never knew you were an expert in Judo and Karate. Who could imagine such delicate, slim and fragile looking girl could outsmart a tall well-built man," said Suri with eyes full of admiration.

"It is good you have shifted from Miss Ranjan's house. The atmosphere stinks there. Think of the immoral relations between her and that dirty fellow Romesh."

"I agree with you. Good riddance," said Pramela.

The teaching work for Pramela was not very heavy but quite tiring. But she had to work for five days in a week with Saturdays and Sundays off. At least she could take rest or visit a friend on these days. She enjoyed her work and was quite satisfied with the general working conditions. The salary was not high and she had to struggle to exist with her salary. But by now Pramela had got accustomed to a rough and tough life. It was a change from her luxurious and carefree life before father's death. In her work she enjoyed being in the midst of tiny tots and this more than compensated for the discomforts.

On the first weekend she spent quite some time on improving the get-up of the small bed-cum-sitting room. It was cheap but clean and had attendant service. She could cook on a gas stove. This room formed her home. She tried to eradicate the drabness and put some life into the room. She put a framed water-colour painting of a landscape, a photograph of her parents, a pair of brocade curtains, a few books and magazines and a China flower pot with fresh flowers.

Tarun had sent her a beautiful pink rug to cover the old worn out carpet. Savvy brought her a charming satin cushion and bone-china tea set. Suri sent fresh flowers almost every two or three days, flowers of all types, mores of all sizes and colours, carnations etc. He knew her liking for roses and made it a point to include a lot of roses too. The small shabby room now got transformed into an attractive one which helped Pramela get over any feelings of depression or unhappiness.

Tarun fixed a program with Pramela for the coming Saturday evening. She was supposed to go for a movie and dinner with him. She had, however, gotten very tired from the effort she had put up in decorating her room. She preferred now to stretch herself in her bed and relax. But an evening out with Tarun was quite tempting. He had already booked seats in the theatre for a new movie.

But the temptation of the evening's rest was so compelling that she finally decided to call Tarun and cancel the program.

She went to the telephone booth in the hall close to her room and called up Tarun and said "I am sorry; I don't think I can keep my engagement, Tarun."

"My dear," said Tarun. "Anything wrong?"

His voice, full of concern, amused her and she said laughingly, "Nothing serious, I am just tired due to the day's work."

"Oh only that, I got worried to death. I shall be at your room in no time and meet you," he said and hung up without giving her any time to reply.

Twenty minutes later, Tarun was in her room, sitting on one of the chairs talking to her while she was cuddled up on her bed.

"You worry unnecessarily, Tarun," started Pramela. "It is only that I am too tired to go out."

"But you shouldn't strain yourself. All this work may be done gradually," said Tarun. "You could have called me."

Pramela looked at the handsome face of Tarun turn pale with worry. She realized how much he adored her. Any other girl would be too happy to reciprocate his love. But she loved Suri and it was well understood that they will marry soon.

"I just need some rest and I shall be all right," said Pramela.

"You have already bought tickets for the movie. Why waste the same? Why not take somebody else?" said Pramela.

"Oh, forget about the tickets. I don't want to take any other person but you. You know that," said Tarun with a slight frown.

"Take Suman along, she loves you Tarun and she is efficient. I am sure she would make a good wife," said Pramela to tease him.

"I harbour no such feelings towards her. Question of me marrying her does not arise."

"But it is time you get married," said Pramela.

At this moment Tarun so much wanted to say that he loved her from the bottom of his heart and would marry no one else. But he constrained himself not to speak of his heart. He simply said in a matter of fact way, "The girl I want to marry won't have me. So I shall not marry any one."

Pramela could understand the emotional agony he was feeling. She preferred to let the matter stay at that. To ease the hurt she said, "I am sure I shall also never marry."

"You can't say that way; you are so young and lovely. You certainly will have plenty of suitors," said Tarun.

"I shall be twenty two next week."

"I never realized that. Are you throwing a birthday party?" asked Tarun.

"I can have one maybe with a small group of friends in this very room. You, Savvy and Suri shall be the sole participants."

Tarun's face fell at the very mention of Suri. His heart swelled with jealously but he managed to control his feelings and regain his composure almost instantaneously.

"Pramela, you are turning twenty two. Time seems to fly," said Tarun. "But I am sure it is my privilege to throw a birthday party for you."

"But the turbulence recently in my life has prematurely aged me. I feel middle aged."

"What rubbish. You still look fresh and young like a budding flower."

Pramela looked at his face and said, "since when have you turned to be a poet?"

"Maybe it's because of the infections company of my little Pramela."

"I prefer you in this happy mood, making you look young and charming. But it is time you leave for the movie if you do not want to miss it."

"I am not going for the movie any more," said Tarun. "It is either with you or none."

"You care so much for me? I feel flattered."

"If you have finally decided not to go, I will better run home. I had some important business in hand," said Tarun.

"But you came here leaving all that business?" enquired Pramela.

"Coming here has been more rewarding. But you are too tired; I will forego that pleasure and prefer you to enjoy your well-deserved rest."

"I am resting all right. If you are not in a hurry, I will love to talk with you for the rest of the evening," said Pramela in an unprecedented feeling of good will for him.

"I will love that but only if I do not bore you. You know, I am more a matter of fact person and not a fluent talker," said Tarun dejectedly.

"Silence is more voluminous than sound, my dear Tarun," said Pramela. "Rest assured; I will enjoy every moment, you sitting here, talking or just being silent."

So Tarun and Pramela continued their conversation for another couple of hours mostly revisiting the incidences of the past, right from their childhood to the present. Time flew rapidly and it was well past 9 pm when Tarun ultimately preceded to take her leave.

"I don't feel like going, leaving you here all alone," said Tarun.

"I shall not be alone. Memory of our pleasant evening shall be with me," said Pramela.

He gave no reply, just looked at her lovely face with all the tenderness at his command. He was in a light mood and filled with romance. But, being shy by nature, he could not fully cash in the opportunity to win over her heart.

If Pramela had simply once said "stay," he would have

jumped on the opportunity and proposed to her. But she had said nothing. He simply smiled and had no option but to leave.

Suddenly it occurred to Tarun that she has not taken her dinner. Perhaps he could order one from a restaurant nearby or they could go out for dinner.

"What about your dinner?" asked Tarun. "Sorry, I had completely forgotten about that."

"I don't feel like taking dinner," said Pramela. "Oh, come on. I will take you to a nearby *dhaba* (eating place) called '*Sardar da Dhaba*' (eating place owned by a Sikh man) where the food is excellent, the place is reasonably neat and clean and service is fast," proposed Tarun.

Pramela agreed to it reluctantly. Within five minutes they were at the dhaba. This being the peak hour, the hall was full to the brim. They had to wait for about five minutes before they got a small table in a corner. Tarun ordered some beer and food for dinner. He knew that Pramela took only beer and no other liquor. Food was served just at the time when they had finished with their beer. As expected, the food was excellent, better than that offered in any good hotel. Tarun paid the bill and soon they were back to her room. Pramela by now was in a hilarious mood.

"I hope you enjoyed your food," asked Tarun.

"It was excellent. More important was the company," said Pramela on the spur of the moment.

"That is true for me also. May I look forward to more such occasions?" remarked Tarun.

"You are a dear one, Tarun. I shall call you one evening. Meanwhile would you care for a cup of steaming hot coffee?" asked Pramela.

Tarun looked at her with pleasure and surprise. She had been unusually considerate with him that evening.

"I shall eagerly await a call from you, dear Pramela and shall certainly relish a cup of coffee now prepared by you."

Pramela was very favourably disposed towards him just then. She had thoroughly enjoyed his company. She mentally compared him with Vicky who had mauled her spirit. On the other hand, Tarun, she thought, was highly reliable, honest and helpful. Further she found that evening that he could be a very charming person once he came out of his usual quiet demeanour. This she attributed to the nature of his profession. There is an extremely tender heart under a thick layer of artificial cover. All she had to do was to reach the inner core and establish a rapport. She wondered how deceptive sometimes are the exterior appearances and false gestures. She was lost in thought.

"I am awaiting your coffee dear. You are lost somewhere. Are you thinking of Suri," said Tarun teasing her.

"Frankly speaking, at the moment I have been thinking of you."

"I feel greatly honoured, dear Pramela, by being engaged in your thoughts. Are you by chance comparing me with Vicky or Major Surjeet? Vicky has proved to be a scoundrel. As far as Surjeet is concerned, I do not compare favourably," said Tarun teasing her.

To his further surprise, Pramela remarked.

"You are right Tarun. Vicky has proved to be a scoundrel. Suri is a dear one undoubtedly. But we are yet to decide."

"And how chivalrously are you disposed towards me," said Tarun teasing her again.

But Pramela was dead serious. "As I said, you are dear, competent, trustworthy, dependable and helpful. Today I was able to probe into your charming heart thoroughly which is encased under your exterior professional personality," said Pramela.

"I am happy you have considered me worthy of your kind attention," said Tarun jokingly. "Shall I consider it as an outing that came to your expectations?"

Actually he wanted to say "shall I consider it as a proposal" but being reserved till this very moment, he didn't allow himself to put his cards openly. He was afraid of rejection. He further argued mentally that he had already indirectly put forth his proposal. It was up to her to respond.

Pramela so much wanted to say "yes." But she could not. There was a conflict going on in her mind. She preferred to postpone the issue.

"You are extremely high in my esteem," Pramela said avoiding a direct answer to the question. "I shall prepare coffee and be there in a minute."

Once the coffee was over, Tarun took her leave and went home.

After he left, Pramela collapsed in a heap on her bed and wept bitterly. She wondered why she couldn't follow what her heart said and couldn't respond to Tarun's hints. Her old reticence and perhaps a little conceit had come in her way. She thought she had missed the opportunity for better or for worse.

Next day was a Sunday. She wanted to take complete rest. She picked up a novel, one of many that Savvy had sent to her, and kept herself busy. In the afternoon she went out to do a bit of shopping. When she reached her place, she saw a beautiful Esteem car with light metal blue colour parked outside the house. She recognized it as Suri's recently purchased car. She tried to guess why he was there at that time of the day.

The daily help, Prabha appeared from nowhere and said, "Major Surjeet is in madam's parlour waiting to see you." "Well I look all messed up from heat and dirt. I will dress up in five minutes time. Then please send Major Surjeet in."

Five minutes later, Pramela greeted Suri in her room "It is indeed a surprise, seeing you at this time of the day," said Pramela. "Nothing specific I believe."

"It was such a hot and tiring day. I thought, I may as well meet you and later take you out for some dinner and dance."

"I have just returned from the market," Pramela told him.

Suri looked at her with admiration in his eyes.

"You look very attractive," he said.

"The attraction is in the beholder's eye, or so is the saying," said Pramela, "The truth is, I look pretty shady because of the dust and dirt."

"For once I beg to differ from you on this account. You indeed look charming despite the dust and dirt," he said.

"To differ with grace needs a special acumen, to concern is so simple," said Pramela.

"You flatter me."

"Flattery does pay most of the time, isn't that true?" she said.

"I have no option but to agree," said Suri. "All through today I was looking forward for the evening with you. You make such a difference in my life."

"I equally enjoy the evenings out with you."

"So get ready soon and we will go out."

"I will bathe and get ready soon. But you must wait in the parlour as I will get dressed here."

Pramela had a hurried bath and wore a light make up. She put on a lemon coloured silk *saree* and a pure gold designer necklace. When she stepped out Suri looked up at her with admiration.

"You look extremely enchanting in this wear," he said. "A perfect model of a nursery school teacher."

"This is one of the *sarees* I had bought for myself before the financial crisis," said Pramela.

"It matches your complexion and you look so lovely like a fairy from Indralok."

"Oh, please don't shower superfluous praise. I am just what I am," said Pramela.

"Let us not go anywhere. We will sit and talk. They both came to her room," suggested Suri.

He looked directly into her eyes with extreme longing and found that her eyes spoke the same language. He could no longer wait. He took her fingers, pressing gently, carried them to his lips. She gave no resistance. Suddenly he burst out.

"I love you Pramela, I love you madly. I knew it from the moment I set my eyes on you at Jabalpur. It is so silly of me, that I took so long to tell you. I can't live without you. Will you marry me? Of course, I won't take no for an answer."

He was breathing heavily and his face was flushed. Pramela skin was also warm as if on fire. She became completely speechless and allowed him to embrace her in his arms. He was now holding her close to him and tightening his grip passionately. She realised that she could hardly breathe. She was equally moved by the rage of love burning within her. All other senses went numb; gradually she lifted her lips and buried them in his lips sucking all the pleasure she could. Time seemed to stand still.

When he finally released her, he knew his love for her had been reciprocated. He felt as if he was walking in the seventh heaven. What more could he ask for in life?

"My dearest Pramela, my sweet little thing, will you marry me?" He repeated with a stammer in his voice.

"I would love to but...," she said, still in her intoxicated state.

"No ifs or buts. I will not take no for an answer. You have to say yes," he interrupted.

"But you have to consider my current financial position," she murmured.

"That is immaterial. I am interested in you and not your money or financial status or your status in the society. I have a steady job and in addition, I have property yielding me a good income. We can have a comfortable if not a luxurious life."

Pramela had been anticipating a proposal from Suri but not so early. She was in fact not mentally prepared for it. The memory of deceit by Vicky constantly lingered in her mind. She in her good days had prepared herself to face disgrace by marrying Vicky, simply for the sake of love. But there was no love on Vicky's part, just a well planned scheme to possess her and her finances. Then there was Tarun, always very helpful and reliable and who had almost proposed to her yesterday. Now her thoughts turned to Suri; nice, sincere and dependable person. But could she love him as naturally and as violently as she had loved Vicky? But what had resulted from her love for Vicky, nothing but frustration and malice; finally she had been deceived. Perhaps she was not a good judge of human nature, of men, their capacity for love, devotion and sacrifice. She was a bit uncertain and lost in thoughts. The fabric of her thought was torn by Suri's voice, "Oh Pramela, please answer me, say that you will marry me? Surely there is no one else in your life other than me. Isn't that true?"

"No one," she replied. She had discounted Tarun as she always thought Tarun was not truly in love with her. He cared for her, out of pity and out of a sense of loyalty to the family.

But yesterday's incident gave her an impression that perhaps Tarun also loved her truly but was only hesitant in expressing it in a manner that Suri had done, and she felt confused. With an effort, she pushed Tarun's thought out of her mind.

She felt that the present was certainly true. Suri loved her enormously and she on her part, found him charming and sincere. She had just felt a great pleasure and thrill when Suri had encircled her in his arms and expressed his deep love for her.

With grace she succumbed to the present situation, looked in his eyes and said,

"Do you really love me so much and long to marry me as I am?"

"I love you as humanly as is possible and long to marry you and be with you till the death parts us," he said lovingly.

"I love you too. But once I loved Vicky, much more deeply and I feel that I will never be able to love anyone in that magnitude," said Pramela.

"But I assure you; eventually you will love me even more. I promise I will never betray you, my sweet Pramela."

"I don't know, I have been ditched once and I feel so insecure," said Pramela with tears in her eyes.

Suri took her hand and said,

"Please give me a chance. Have faith in me."

"I have complete faith in you. But I am afraid of another betrayal and that will lead me to my funeral. I am broken from inside," said Pramela making an unsuccessful effort to check the outburst of tears followed by uncontrolled sobbing.

"Don't cry, my sweet Pramela. You have my word of honour; I will do everything possible to keep you happy. Just say that you will marry me."

"I will, if you really want me," said Pramela.

"My sweet Pramela, I am so happy," he could hardly say it as his voice was hoarse with emotion. He embraced her again and gave her a long endearing kiss.

Pramela now realized that she stood engaged to be

married to Suri and a sense of deep happiness and love swelled in her.

"Let us celebrate this occasion," said Suri enthusiastically, Pramela was only too willing. They drove to an excellent hotel retreat, little away from the main city located off the national highway. The place was quiet and patronized by its special customers. Suri ordered for a special celebration dinner preceded with the best champagne available. Both Suri and Pramela were intoxicated more from their love for one another than the drink.

By the time they had finished their dinner, both were in a state of extreme joy. Pramela had finally decided to marry Suri at the earliest and start her life afresh. She had already suffered too much during these last few months and Suri readily agreed to it. He was also keen to have her as his wife.

"Let us marry as soon as we can and have a long honeymoon," proposed Suri. "We can go to any hill station you prefer; Shimla, Mussorie, Dalhousie or Pachhmarhi."

"I suggest we go to Pachhmarhi. It has its scenic beauty; multiple places to visit and is relatively quiet. We do need a quiet and a comfortable place for ourselves, don't we."

So it was all decided.

"We must tell Tarun about our engagement," said Pramela.

"Yes, we must tell him first," he agreed.

"I will call him first thing in the morning," said Pramela. "I am sure he will be surprised by the recent development."

"I hope he approves, he is a sort of an unofficial guardian to me, I suppose."

"Tarun is a dear one and a good friend indeed. He will certainly approve of our engagement," said Pramela.

Suri let go of Tarun from his mind and confined himself to thoughts of his future life with Pramela.

Pramela, on the other hand, could not remove the thoughts of Tarun from her mind, perhaps because of her long association with him and his visit to her room yesterday. She argued with herself that she must remove all thoughts about Tarun from her mind, since she was now engaged to Suri in a sense.

Pramela knew that once she was married to Suri, he would manage her affairs and she will more or less lose contact with Tarun. She felt uneasy at this thought but that is what she must do. Perhaps she might have to go abroad once Suri accepted the permanent commission. Alternatively Suri may start some business in Delhi itself. All possibilities were in the melting pot. She knew that she would be happy with him whatever his position, and she vowed that she would endeavour to keep him happy in every possible way.

She got deeply lost in thoughts about her future life as Suri's wife. She realized that all of a sudden things change and girls do look forward to a happy married life. But they also seem disinclined to leave their old surroundings and old companions.

"You are lost in thought, darling," said Suri. "Anything worrying you?"

"No nothing dear, just contemplating on my future with you. I am mentally prepared for the marriage and will marry you whenever you prefer."

"My sweet Pramela, what a difference you have made in my life by accepting my proposal. I am certainly the luckiest person in this world," said Suri.

They kept talking and planning their future until it was well past midnight. Finally they returned to Pramela's lodge. Suri was not in a state of mind to leave. However, Pramela persuaded him to be sensible.

"Tomorrow we will go and choose the engagement

ring," said Suri. "I will talk to my parents and fix a formal engagement ceremony."

"Whatever you say is ok with me," is all she could say.

It had started raining and the roads had become slippery. Pramela cautioned him to drive slowly to his residence. Reluctantly they parted.

Pramela walked into her bedroom in an intoxicated state. It was less from the consumption of champagne and from the events of the night. She intently listened to the sound of the car receding from the lodge.

Slowly she changed her clothes and stretched herself on the bed. But sleep eluded her. The thoughts of her future life dominated her mind. She decided that she would inform both Savvy and Tarun in the morning. Later, she would write to Bua Radha, the Kansal couple and Tara at Jabalpur. Engaged in such thoughts, she ultimately surrendered to sleep.

Next day Pramela got up at the usual time, though the hectic schedule of the previous night caused her body to ache.

She decided to take off from work that day.

That morning when she called up Tarun to tell him about all that happened, his heart missed a beat. He listened to her quietly as it was always a pleasure listening to her.

"I must speak to you," said Pramela excitedly. "I am so happy."

"Give me the good news."

"It is wonderful," said Pramela. "I am engaged to be married."

"Many congratulations. I think, I guessed it right."

"You know it's Suri."

His face fell. He knew it could be none other than Suri. He now knew that he had lost the opportunity. Perhaps it was so destined, he thought. "How lucky Suri is." He tried to recompose himself , "Please let me know, if I can be of any help for you and Suri. But, I would like to talk to you. Will you have lunch with me? We will talk over the lunch."

"I wish I could, but I am having lunch with Suri."

"Then can you make it at any time convenient to you, say before the lunch?"

"That suits me. I will reach your office by about 11 am," said Pramela and terminated the call.

Tarun was in a state of great frustration with Pramela as she was marrying Suri. He saw the implication; Pramela will go away from Delhi. She would be going from place to place where Suri would be required to serve. He won't be able to meet her or even talk to her. Even this privilege would be denied to him. He was wild with anger.

Tarun tried to distract his mind from the thoughts of Pramela and tried in vain to concentrate on his work. He waited for Pramela to come.

Time passed beyond 11 am and Pramela did not appear. For him time dragged at a miserably slow pace. Every two or three minutes he looked at his watch. At 12 noon, he lost hope and called Pramela's lodge. He was told that Miss Pramela was in her room. He felt a bit annoyed. But he politely requested the land lady to tell Pramela that Mr. Tarun Gupta wanted to and speak with her.

"I will tell her if you like," said the land lady, Mrs. Kapoor. "But I am sure she will not come. She has a bad news. Miss Savvy and one captain Sharma are with her. Her friend ..."

Tarun interrupted the call. The news that Pramela was in trouble was good enough reason for Tarun to leave immediately for her lodge. He could not make out what was wrong. He should have fully listened to the landlady. The only thought in his mind was to help Pramela out of her present situation.

After Pramela had called Tarun, she had remained in her room whiling away her time. She expected a call from Suri by 11 am but she did not get any call. A little later, she heard a car stop before her lodge. It was not Suri's car. It belonged to Suri's friend Captain Sharma. Moments later, Captain Sharma and Savvy entered her room. Pramela was delighted to see Savvy and greeted her, however her enthusiasm died when she saw their grave faces.

"What is the matter? Is anything wrong?" Pramela asked.

"Yes, darling," said Savvy. "Something very grave has happened."

"Please do tell me. I am so worried now," said Pramela.

None of the two visitors had the courage to disclose the truth. Finally Savvy, with tears filled in her eyes, whispered, "Pramela darling, it must be a ghastly shock to you. But I have no choice but to tell you that Suri will not be able to see you again."

Pramela now realized that something very serious had happened to Suri.

"What is the matter with Suri. Is he serious ill? What do you mean by not able to see me again?" Pramela said, greatly disturbed.

"I don't know how to break the news to you."

"Is he seriously ill?" again asked Pramela, a little impatiently.

Savvy could not possibly tell her. She turned to Capt. Sharad Sharma.

She said to Sharma, "Please tell Pramela, I possibly can't."

Capt. Sharma gradually turned to face Pramela, "I am awfully sorry to give this bad news. Last night after Suri returned home from your lodge, he fell seriously ill."

"Tell me how is he now? What is the illness?" asked Pramela.

"He had a massive heart attack and he was shifted to the hospital at once."

"But you don't have heart attacks at this age."

"Yes, that is true. But exceptions are there. It was in his family. His uncle died of heart attack at a very young age," said Capt. Sharma.

"But in the army you have regular medical checkups. He must have known," enquired Pramela.

"Yes, there was a very slight trouble. He was advised to avoid very strenuous work. Perhaps he was afraid he would be declared medically unfit. That is why, despite his reluctance for regular commission, he was contemplating a civilian job or some business."

"I see," said Pramela thoughtfully. "But how is he now? Why did he not send a word for me? I must go to him at once."

"Please wait," said Sharma gently, putting a hand on her shoulder.

"Suri knew that he won't last long. I was called to be with him. He did not want you to suffer. He told me about your marriage promise. It was a great shock for all of us."

"Do you mean… is Suri dead?" cried Pramela.

"It was destined. All the efforts that were made to save him were in vain. Then I called Savvy and we both came here to inform you."

"Did he remember me?"

"Yes, he was very disturbed about you. He wanted you to carry on as a brave person and not to grieve on his account."

Pramela was in a terrible shock and stood speechless thinking over the cruelty of destiny.

"I was going to write to you about my marriage Savvy this afternoon," Pramela said slowly. "But the entire pleasure has been snatched away from me."

Savvy stood weeping bitterly on the misfortune of her

dear friend.

"Did he suffer too much?" asked Pramela.

"He had an acute pain but all necessary medicines were given. But he had a peaceful end."

I was near him in his last moments he knew you were brave. But at the same time he did not want you to see the suffering of a dying man. "He wanted me to convey his love to you."

"Thank you captain Sharma for being at his side during his parting moments. Only memories remain for me and of course you all."

"His parents were all the time with him. It was a great consolation," said Sharma.

"When is the funeral?"

"Suri had specifically asked me to convey that you should not attend his funeral and not to participate in any kind of mourning," said Sharma.

Pramela kept sitting, completely dumb found. Savvy and Capt. Sharma also kept quiet. Savvy tried to console her but Pramela told her that she wanted to be alone for the time being.

Savvy also preferred to let her alone for some time. Before leaving however, Savvy said, "Pramela, call me whenever you need me."

"I will do that," murmured Pramela.

"I am leaving now and will be back again," said Savvy.

Capt. Sharma and Savvy took her leave.

"I will also see you again," he said. "Please do not hesitate to call me if you need anything."

Capt. Sharma and Savvy left for their car. Ever since Savvy was introduced to Capt. Sharma, both had developed a liking for each other and had been meeting quite frequently.

Both were deeply struck by this calamity. Sharma had lost a good friend while Savvy felt sad for her best friend Pramela.

Once they reached the car, Sharma invited Savvy to have lunch with him. After lunch, Savvy asked him to leave her again at Pramela's lodge.

"She is all alone," she said. "By now she must have cried some of her sorrow out and she may need some company."

"You are so thoughtful Savvy," he said. "Come, I will drop you there."

"When is the cremation?" she asked.

"They will have to wait for the arrival of his brother from Bangalore. He will arrive by the first available flight.

"Suri's parents have only him left now."

They started for Pramela's place and by then Tarun had reached Pramela's place too. He saw her crying and asked her;

"What is the bad news? You have been crying, don't you?"

"It is about Suri," answered Pramela.

"What about him?"

"This morning he had a massive heart attack and he passed away. His parents and his friend Capt. Sharma were by his side in the hospital when he last breathed."

"You mean he is dead?" asked Tarun.

"Yes, Suri is dead."

"Oh my lord," said Tarun.

Then Pramela gave him all the details. Tarun remained completely nonplussed, listening patiently to the incident narrated by Pramela.

"O my God, such a horrible luck. Suri died when we had just finally decided to marry you.

"It is awful…!" said Tarun. "Suri died at such young age. It will be equally shocking to his parents."

"He was so young, smart and full of life," added Pramela.

The news was highly shocking to Tarun too. But he felt sorry for Pramela, who was completely broken by this sad news. He could see that she was deeply suffering from this sudden calamity although she had regained her calm and composure.

Tarun remained quiet for some time. Finally he found courage to console her.

"I do not have words to console you," said Tarun in a low tone. "But I must say that I am shocked to the core of my heart and deeply sympathise with you."

"I draw courage from friends like you and Savvy. But I have a rotten luck. First my father's death, then the financial ruin, next the deceit by Vicky and now finally this death. I don't know what sin I have committed to deserve all this?"

"Oh dear Pramela, don't accuse yourself. You are simply not capable of committing any sin. You are so simple and pure. But then God has his own ways of dealing with people giving pleasures and pains to all of us."

"Suri had also wished that I should not attend his funeral, not grieve over his death unduly and just carry on with my life," said Pramela.

"I agree with the first part of his wish. You should not attend the funeral. But not to grieve over the death will be rather difficult. However as time passes, you will tend to reduce the grief and get stronger," said Tarun.

"Yes, time is the healer," said Pramela. "Also, I will continue to work as per his wishes. It is more necessary from his point of view that I earn a livelihood and to keep my mind engaged."

"I tend to agree with you," responded Tarun. "But how can you continue under the present condition?"

"I will take off, may be for a fortnight and then come back to work."

"I must face life as it comes. If only unhappiness is my share of luck, I must reconcile to it," said Pramela.

Tarun had no answer. He had all the sympathy for her. He simply looked at her with pity. Her eyes met his look and she could measure the feeling of co-suffering in it. She felt that her suffering was unduly putting him in pain too. She moved towards him, held his hand and said, "My dear Tarun, please don't strain yourself on my account. I can definitely overcome the present grief and will be alright soon."

Tarun pressed her hands, a gesture of being an equal partner in the present grief.

"I wish I could do something to see you happy," he said.

"Dear Tarun, only thing I would like you to do is to be my friend and to give me strength to bear this loss."

"You can depend on me," said Tarun. "But you have to abide by my wishes, for a change."

"I shall do anything to overcome the grief."

"Change of place is a good healer. I would like you to come and live with us for a few days and don't say no," pressed Tarun.

Reluctantly she agreed. Tarun helped her pack her suitcase and he took it to the car and drove her to his home.

Pramela found the change of place a welcoming one and invigorating. Suman had gone to stay with a cousin at Aligarh. Both Tarun and his mother did everything possible to divert Pramela's mind from the recent catastrophe. The following week she returned to her lodge and her duty. But as promised she was to spend the week end with Tarun and his mother. She often thought of moving back to Jabalpur but Tarun and his mother persuaded her to stay in Delhi and Pramela did so. She found the atmosphere at Tarun's place very congenial and soothing.

Time passed on. Savvy visited Pramila regularly. Pramela learnt from Savvy about her romance with Capt. Sharma. It was now obvious that they will get engaged soon. Tarun, as a great friend came to her lodge almost every weekend and took her at his home. About eight months passed in this manner and Pramela almost got over the pain inflicted by the sudden death of Suri. She had developed very pleasant relations with Tarun, his mother and his cousin.

One fine evening Savvy came excitedly to Pramela's lodge and announced her engagement with Capt. Sharma.

"I am so happy dear Savvy. This had to happen," said Pramela.

Pramela was again reminded of Suri, their decision of marriage and his sudden death. She was happy, that her closest friend Savvy at least was getting engaged and going in for a blissful married life.

That weekend Pramela told Tarun about the engagement of Savvy with Capt. Sharma. He felt quite happy and called Savvy to congratulate her.

Tarun by now had found a very good rapport with Pramela. She found in him as an excellent friend and companion and thus he was responsible for easing the tension and misery from her life caused by the death of Suri. For this gesture she felt greatly indebted to him. Tarun, on his part, made every possible effort to make her life easier and cheerful and carefully avoided unnecessary arguments and unpleasant situations. At the same time he always preferred her to take her own decisions and be independent.

Quite often Tarun would take Pramela out for dinner and dance. He was a poor dancer but to please Pramela he made concrete efforts to learn the steps involved in various dances. Soon he started to enjoy dancing too. Pramela, on the other hand, always loved to dance and would dance for long hours. To his own surprise, he found that he could by now dance well as he was light on his feet and had an excellent sense of rhythm. To dance with Pramela as a period of extreme happiness and satisfaction for him. Pramela also felt more at ease while dancing with him. Now Pramela had gradually changed the life style of Tarun. When they danced, almost all eyes turned to them and they made an excellent pair. On many occasions, girls sought to dance with Tarun and he did dance with them but he always preferred Pramela. Earlier Tarun never used to take hard drinks, not even beer. But with more social gatherings, he had started enjoying beer which he would consume in a generous manner. Often he would take a peg of whisky or two too.

"I am afraid, I am spoiling you, dear Tarun," said Pramela one evening.

They had completed one round of dance and preferred to sit at a table to take rest and talk. Others wanted to dance with her, but she politely declined and got seated by his side.

"I am afraid, I have spoilt you into dancing and drinks, dear Tarun," said Pramela, teasing him.

"For once you are wrong, Pramela darling," said Tarun. "In fact I have learnt to enjoy dance, drink and club life and I am obliged to you for this."

"Have you realized Tarun that you are more open now and smile at the tiniest opportunity?" she said.

"You are a different person altogether."

"I must again attribute it to your good influence." He smiled and said, "I feel at least five years younger."

"Yes, you can compete with any young man in his early twenties," she said teasingly.

"You are accelerating things and pulling my legs."

"No I am not. Have you ever realized how handsome and attractive you look when you smile," she said and he blushed like a boy and said,

"I don't know. But I have certainly changed, may be for good or for bad, I don't know."

"The girls dote on you. Haven't you seen the look in their eyes? I am sure any of them would jump to marry you if you give a slightest indication," she said further.

"I am not interested in just any girl," he said a little indifferently.

"Who is the specific girl you are interested in, Tarun?"

"You know that, don't you?"

"I wish I knew," she said calmly.

But she knew what he meant. He was, however, too conscious to propose for the fear of it being turned down. Pramela, on the other hand, had started liking him to the point where she could accept a proposal from him. A barrier had, however, got created, and it was too difficult to break. Perhaps someday, both may be in a more liberal disposition!

Pramela was glad however, she had in a way taught Tarun to be more free, open and interesting. Even Suman had changed. Earlier she was jealous of Pramela who was the centre of attention for Tarun. But of late, Suman had given up her idea of attracting Tarun into matrimony. A young social worker now got her attention. Soon the two got married and Suman started living with him.

Pramela continued with her job at the school and lived at the lodge. One morning as she was preparing to go to the school, when the maid came running to her.

"Phone call for you, miss."

On the phone, she heard Tarun's voice.

"I want to meet you this evening without fail," he said.

"Is it important?" she asked. "I was going for a drive this evening with my principal."

"Put it off, my dear Pramela," persuaded Tarun.

"Is anything serious?"

"No, nothing" he said. "Only that I am required to go to Bombay for about a fortnight and I want to talk to you about it."

"Going on business?"

"Yes, on business our firm has an important client and they need our presence," he said.

With a shock she realized that she did not want Tarun to go , not even for a week. She, off late, was meeting him almost every other day and she realized with a shock that she was enjoying his company. It occurred to her that life in Delhi without him would be extremely drab and a week's time was too much. She questioned herself whether she was in love with him. Perhaps yes. It was like a gift from heaven. She must probe her heart fully and further probe the response of Tarun. She was lost in her thoughts. It was the voice of Tarun that brought her to the present.

"Are you there?" Tarun asked.

"I am, yes, very much. I will cancel my appointment and meet you in the evening."

"Nice girl. Let's meet at the hotel at seven."

"I will be there. Good-bye," she said.

"And yes, I would rather come and pick you and take you there. Be ready by about 6.30 pm," he said and hung up.

She got ready a little early. He arrived precisely at half past six and was all dressed up.

"You look very alluring," he remarked.

"I try to keep myself fit," she remarked casually.

She was eager to know more about the proposed visit.

Tarun placed himself on one of the chairs and said, I am going to Bombay on business and will be required to stay there for a function for a fortnight. My client is a rich man. He wants me to make it a business cum pleasure trip. He has planned to go to Goa by a chauffer driven car. I hope it will be a pleasant change."

"I envy you," she said teasingly.

"I am not keen. But this client is pressing too hard and insists that I must have a break from routine."

"You do deserve a change after all the hard work you are putting up with," she said.

"I wondered if you could join me in the trip."

"I would be only too glad. But you know I can't afford this luxury," she said a little dejectedly.

"I wondered if you could join me as a business associate say as my secretary," he added with hesitation. "Then the entire expenses would be borne by the client."

Pramela desperately wanted to accompany him and did not want to miss the opportunity.

"I would only be glad to join you as your secretary," she said. "Just that I don't look as good as a secretary."

"What? you definitely look like a beautiful secretary my darling," he said in a romantic mood. "You will more than compensate by your mere presence."

"Oh Tarun, you are wonderful. I am so happy," she said clutching his arms.

Her closeness to his body and the spark in her eyes were too intoxicating for Tarun to control his emotions. He desperately tried to control himself but in vain. His breathing became heavy and his face turned pale.

"What is the matter, Tarun?" asked Pramela.

"Can't you see how you affect me emotionally? I lose my control. I can't trust myself with you."

"What a change? You are so self-controlled and sedate. What caused such a change?" asked Pramela.

"Why don't you understand Pramela? If there was any other girl it would not matter to me at all. But you are Pramela, the girl I love, love too much to take a chance of travelling with you and just maintaining a platonic relationship," said Tarun.

He was now perspiring all over.

Significance of his outburst dawned on Pramela gradually. So he had finally expressed his deep love for her in his own way, a rather unusual way. But the fact penetrated her heart. Tarun was deeply in love with her. She on her part had also developed a liking for him. Do I love him? She questioned herself. Surprisingly the answer was yes. Why had she got so disturbed when he declared his fortnight's tour?

Having assessed the situation, she looked directly into his eyes as if to assess the truth of this new revelation.

She realized now how deeply he had loved her for a long time, from the time her father was alive. But she did not trust his love since it was not reciprocated in her heart then.

He had seen through the treacherous designs of Vicky. He had remained a selfless friend, even after the death of Suri. Perhaps it was too much for his self-control now. His love was real, selfless, devoted sacrificing and asking for nothing in return. She got overwhelmed with the love for him. She stretched herself as if to tell him how much she loved him too.

Tarun wiped the perspiration from his forehead with the handkerchief and met her gaze.

"Pramela darling, I am sorry that I have made a mess." Tarun said apologetically.

"No you haven't, you have expressed your deep love for me. I am so happy that finally you opened your heart to me."

"You don't mean that. Do you mean you care a bit for me?" asked Tarun excitedly.

"You say just a bit! No it is lots Tarun. Just that I could not express it and incidentally nor could you."

Tarun suddenly cheered up. He caught both her hands and slowly brought them to his lips. She did not object to it.

"Pramela darling, you have made me the happiest man in the world. How can I thank you for it? I know I don't deserve you but now promise that you will be mine forever."

"Oh Tarun, I love you and would love to be with you all the time. I can't bear to miss you for a fortnight. I would marry right now if that is needed for going on the trip with you," said Pramela. "But please tell me when did you really start loving me?"

"I have always loved you," said Tarun. "But how could I open profess my love for you when you were courting

Vicky and then Suri. Even after the sad demise of Suri, I could not gather courage to propose to you. It is only today I blurted out because of the exigency of the situation. How could I trust myself with self control with a sweet girl as Pramela when she is my sole companion? It was an impossible situation."

"In that case, I must thank your client for providing this situation. Do remind me to thank him when we meet."

"Now Pramela darling, do tell me when did you start liking me, I mean in this way."

"I have always liked you as a reliable, trustworthy and sincere person but it is only lately that I realized that I do love you."

"Pramela darling say it again. My ears love to hear you say so."

"Tarun dear, I love you. I wish I had known this earlier. I have loved two persons in my life but I may say with conviction that I have found a deep, everlasting love now, a love that involves care, sympathy, and sacrifice, a love which reverberates with every movement of body and every thought of mind."

Tarun closed his eyes, visualizing sparks of love radiating from her. His happiness crossed all bounds and slowly he spoke,

"My sweet Pramela, it is difficult to believe this is true, it is too sublime to be granted to an undeserving man."

"Don't say so, Tarun dear. In fact I have been a fool all this while not to have realized your true love, not demanding anything in return from me."

"I am a simple man and I can simply say that I will do anything and everything to keep you happy, my sweet little Pramela."

"I have missed happiness twice. But God has been kind

enough to grant me you. I cannot possibly stand another tragedy," said Pramela.

"You shall ever be mine," said Tarun. "Now get ready for our courting in Bombay and Goa. On return we will get married with no delay and I shall celebrate my ultimate triumph."

"Not yours alone, but our ultimate triumph," corrected Pramela.

"I will humbly get that corrected," said Tarun raising her two arms to embrace her forever.

true, it is
granted to a

" Don't

" You shall ev
ready for our court
return we will estab
immediat get marr
celebrate my ultim

" Y

## ABOUT THE AUTHOR

**Prof. G. K. MITHAL** was a well-known academician and author in the field of Electronics Engineering. He has over a dozen technical books in the field of Electronics and Telecommunication to his credit and was among the first few Indian authors in the field. Many of his books written many decades ago are still bestsellers. He served as a professor in Government Engineering College, Jabalpur for 35 years.

# CROWD-FUNDERS

*(names listed alphabetically)*

- Abhisaar Chetan Sudhakar
- Akshit Gupta
- Amit Manocha
- Anoop Sharma
- Arpita Sharma
- Ashok Kumar Pandey
- Bhawna Aggarwal
- Bheela Wadehra
- Devanshu Mittal
- Maneesha Gupta
- Nikhil Bohra
- Ravi Kant Arora
- Ravi Mittal
- Ravindra Hari Vaghmarey
- Richa Srivastava
- Richa Yadav
- Rohit Bansal
- Saurabh Mittal
- Shireesh Kumar Rai

# Never too Late

**Prof. G. K. MITHAL**

**Did you like the book ?**

Email your
queries, experiences, and suggestions
to
**saurabh@pblishing.com**

www.ingramcontent.com/pod-product-compliance
Lightning Source LLC
Chambersburg PA
CBHW030338030726
47499CB00003B/822
* 9 7 8 8 1 9 3 3 2 4 8 4 4 *